Light Sapphire Eyes

Kevin Teague

ISBN: 0692266933
ISBN-13: 9780692266939

The moon is still over her shoulder

The stars are still falling above

She never gets one minute older

And he is still falling in love.

CONTENTS

"Doubt that the stars are fire, Doubt that the sun doth move his aides, Doubt truth to be a liar, But never doubt I love."

--William Shakespeare

1

DECEMBER 19TH

I woke up with a groan. That was nothing new. Pain greeted every morning with great enthusiasm. It tends to do that when you are eighty-four years old. The cancer inside me was not helping much. I paid it no mind. Old age would take me long before the cancer had its say.

I have become well accustomed to pain. Long years pass until it becomes an old friend that lingers around long enough until you begin to rely on it. I can handle the physical pain. It is the pain of the heart that hurts the most. I have been unable to escape it. It is wrapped around me as tightly as my own soul.

Each day of my last remaining years have been filled with a brutal sameness. Morning comes with decisions that need to be made. The first of which is whether to rise from my bed or stay there until the end comes. I always chose to get up and face the day. The repeating familiarity was a comfort to me.

Except, this day was different from all the rest.

I glanced at the lone window in my small room. A pink glow was beginning to inch its way around the curtains. It was early morning. Good. I was not yet ready to face the day.

The first day without her.

2

BEGINNING

"I've been watching you."

I was heading toward my school bus when the decidedly feminine voice stopped me in my tracks. I turned to see a pretty girl looking at me with a surprising intensity. She appeared to be about my age, which was sixteen. She was thin, with light brown hair that just touched her shoulders. A perfectly shaped face displayed a small nose and full lips. Her eyes completed the stunning package. They were a vivid light blue that seemed to sparkle in the bright afternoon sunlight. It was if she had some kind of inner light that made them seem brighter than normal eyes.

I was intrigued by what she had said. I could recall her name, but that was about all I knew about her. Other than she was pretty, that is. I decided to try some of my witty repartee on her. "Huh?"

She smiled, and I could just make out the hint of a tiny dimple on her chin. "Yep." She stepped closer and looked up at me. "I'm Kara. I know who you are."

Something stirred deep inside me. I was not quite sure what it meant, but I liked what it was doing to me. I returned her smile. "Why have you been watching me?"

She shrugged. "I just have. I like you."

School had just let out for the day. Students were making their way around us as they headed toward the bus that would take them home. The unseasonably warm spring day would be a blessing to bored teenagers everywhere.

Some of that warmth found its way to my face as I blushed furiously. "You don't even know me." I instantly felt stupid for saying it. I quickly added what I hoped would save me. "I think you're pretty."

The dimple reappeared. "Thanks. You're cute. Would you like to go out with me sometime?"

Her words sent a thrill through my body. I later learned that this directness was part of who she was. It would be her way for her entire life. She did not waste any time. She saw what she wanted and went after it.

I, on the other hand, was at a loss for words. It was not often that a pretty girl wanted to talk to me. I swallowed hard while pretending to think about her question. It gave me the time I needed to formulate a coherent thought. "Yeah, I'd like that."

A loud noise brought my head around to where my bus was parked at the curb. The driver gave me an angry look as she honked the horn again. Most of the other busses were already on their way out of the parking lot.

I looked back at Kara. "I'd better go. When do you want to go out?"

She raised herself up on her toes and gave me a quick peck on the cheek. "Friday night." She began to turn toward her own bus. "We will talk more tomorrow." She flashed another smile before turning away.

Despite my exasperated driver, I could not help but stand there and stare at her as she boarded the bus. I raised my hand to touch my cheek where she had kissed it. There was a first time for everything. My grin nearly split my face in two.

I jumped as the voice next to my ear nearly scared me half to death. "Get your ass on the bus or I'm leaving you."

I turned to see my bus driver giving me the evil eye. She angrily jerked her head towards the bright yellow chariot. I looked over to see faces peering at me through its many windows. The driver shook her head before spinning on her heels and stumping her way back to the bus.

The grin never left my face. "Yes, ma'am."

3

DECEMBER 18TH

They held a birthday party for me today, such as it was. Once past a certain age, birthdays do not seem to matter much to me anymore. A yearly reminder that you could die at any moment is not one of my favorite things.

There was the usual cake and ice cream. It was strange that they served it just after breakfast. I never understood their thinking on that, but that is how things are done around here.

There was only one candle on the cake. No need to create a fire hazard with the appropriate number of candles. The nurses made happy sounds and clapped their hands when I blew out the meager flame. I did not really give a damn. All I wanted was a piece of cake, and following the "routine" was the only way to get it.

The birthday routine consists of the lucky person sitting at the big mahogany table located in the center of the dining hall. Once the nurses have you ensconced in the head seat, every able resident sings Happy Birthday. It is not a pretty sound, but they put their hearts into it, which meant more to me than I thought it would. I did give extra credit to Nelly, who screeched out 'I've Got A Feelin'' as an encore. The classics do indeed live forever.

The Harrison Manor Nursing Home is full of routine. From the moment you wake up, until you go to sleep, there is a precise plan to your day. Deviate from it and you get a stern talking-to from nurse Ferrell. It is funny how when you get old that people tend to treat you like a child.

The final reward for the King of the Day, for two full hours, is possession of the remote control to the Common Room big-screen television. I tried not to let the power go to my head. You would be surprised to learn just how many squabbles break out over which channel should be on. It was not long, however, before I became restless, and abdicated my throne to another.

I struggled to my feet and shuffled my way over to the birthday table. The old ache in my bones followed me like a malevolent shadow. I picked up a piece of cake and headed for the door that led out of the hall. Kara could not make it to the party, so I was going to bring the party to her. I idly wondered if she would remember what happened thirty-four years ago today.

It seems like it takes me longer every day to walk down the hall to her room. The nurses constantly nag me about using a wheelchair, but I refuse every time. I will walk as long as I am able, but I fear those days are numbered.

I reached her door and gave it a soft knock. It was not necessary, but it had become a habit that began when she first came to Harrison Manor. I was not about to change it now.

I glanced into the room and a familiar sight greeted me. Kara lay on her bed. Her head of white hair was propped up by a thick pillow. The green and white bedspread was pulled up to her chin. Her face was thin and pale. A nurse must have turned on the television, as the sounds of a game show drifted across the room. She was not paying any attention to it. She rarely paid attention to anything now. I was the only one who could really bring her around.

She did not look any better today. It was a depressing thought that I have had every day for quite a while. She had been brought here to die, but she battled hard to make it to another day. The cancer, which the doctors told her would claim her life within six months, had been taking its toll on her for more than three years. She inspired me in so many ways.

She had not reacted when I knocked, so I just stood in the doorway and studied her. To me, she was as beautiful as the first time I saw her, sixty-eight years ago. Funny that. Even though the ravages of time can ruin a body, I still see her as she once was. My heart ached for her.

I sighed softly and pushed away my sad thoughts. A big smile was on my face by the time I entered the room and walked to the chair that sat next to her bed. It had been placed there for me when she first arrived, and I have rested my boney ass in it ever since.

It turned out that she was sleeping. I did not want to wake her, so I carefully placed the cake on the nightstand. I grabbed the remote control and turned the off the television. I then closed my eyes and began listening to her breathe. I liked doing that. It reassured me that she was still with me. It also reminded me of the nights when she had slept next to me. I would look at her in the depths of the evening

and marvel at her beauty. Those nights had been too
few and too long ago.

Echoes drifted into the room to mix with the
sound of her. Slow footsteps echoed past the open
door. A murmur of voices drifted haphazardly down
the hall. The click of the air conditioning as it turned
itself on. Soft sounds. Quiet sounds. Haunting
sounds.

I shook myself out of my reverie. Now was not
the time to give in to the sadness. She was with me,
no matter what had happened in the past. Even so, it
would never be enough to make up for so many
years of lost time.

I turned back to find her watching me. Those
light sapphire eyes were transfixed on my face. The
starlight had never left her. She was the one who was
sick, but her face was full of concern for me. She
could read me so well.

A tiny smile lifted her lips. "Deep thoughts
again?" Her voice was forced and faint.

I returned a reassuring smile. "Nah, just visiting
old memories."

"Which ones? Are you remembering our good
times or the ones where you blame yourself for all

your pain and misery?" She coughed. "Feeling depressed again, I take it?"

I never understood how she did that. Still, I lied. "Good ones, of course."

"Liar."

Damn. She *always* knew. I had to change the subject. "How are you feeling?"

Her eyes took on a faraway look. "I feel light, as if I were a cloud, drifting on the wind."

I had always loved her tendency to be lyrical, but I did not like the sound of that. I took her hand and squeezed. "Hey, that's nothing. It's probably the medication. It sometimes makes you lightheaded."

She slowly shook her head. "No, not this time." Her eyes found mine, and with that one look, I knew what she meant. I was as certain as if God had tapped me on the shoulder and whispered it in my ear.

Have you ever had a mountain fall on you? Or twenty? That is what happened to me in that moment. The crushing realization of her words threatened to destroy me. A raging torrent of pain tried to wash me away. Oh God, no.

It took me a while to recover. Kara did not say anything. She knew it had to run its course. She watched with sad eyes as rolling waves of despair crashed upon the shores of my heart. She continued to hold my hand until the painful tide began to recede. Her soft words allowed me to summon enough strength to climb my way up through the rubble and start thinking clearly again.

Her voice was full of sadness. "I know what this will do you, my love. I'm sorry. So sorry. I held on to you as long as I could."

The breath caught in my throat. She had stunned me again. She was dying, yet all she thought about was how it would affect me. The love I felt for her in that moment was incalculable.

I lifted her hand to my lips to kiss it. My teardrops made wet patterns on her skin. "You can't leave me now. Three years doesn't make up for a lifetime. Three years is not enough to show you how much I love you." The tears began to stream down my face.

Her frail hands covered my own. "You gave me your love many years ago. You've shown me that and more these past few years. I have always known that you love me. Never doubt that. Ever."

The love I heard in her voice comforted me a little. She was not done. Her next words stunned me yet again.

"I'm going to sleep now. When I wake up, you're going to take me on a walk in the park. Okay?"

What else could my answer be? "Okay."

I watched as she eased down into sleep. I sat at her side and drifted upon a river of emotion. Love and pain. Ecstasy and despair. It all mixed together in a powerful force that tried to drown me in its icy waters.

The memory flooded into my mind...

4

THE FIRST TIME

Night was settling over the park as we drove through the entrance. The sparsely placed street lamps struggled mightily to illuminate the one-lane road. I glanced across the park and did not see another car. We were definitely alone.

The road curved to the right a short distance past the gate. As I navigated the turn, my eyes followed the downward slope on the left. It was a long plunge that ended at the edge of a large pond. Picnic tables and parking spaces squatted forlornly along the edge of the shore. Further along was a children's playground, its brightly colored playthings motionless in the night.

I took a few left turns and we soon arrived at the location I had scouted a few days earlier. I parked the car in the road, as I did not expect any more traffic this night. I was treating it as if we had a private invitation. There would be hell to pay if anything interrupted us this night.

We stepped out of the car and Kara joined me at the back. I popped the trunk and we each took out a blanket. She looked at me askance as I lifted out the beer cooler. I gave her a conspiratorial smile as I turned and began making my way toward the pond.

I walked over to the lone tree that stood near the water's edge. The base of its trunk was ringed with large white stones. The ground was densely covered with grass. It made a perfect spot in which to lay our blankets.

I was as nervous as I had ever been. "How about here?"

She glanced around briefly before bringing her eyes up to mine. The nearest street lamp was a good distance away, but I could see the smile that played on her face.

"It's perfect."

She looked beautiful. Her face was perfection with her small nose and perfectly rounded chin. A tiny dimple would appear there each time she smiled. Her light brown hair hung in easy waves to her shoulders. The sight of her was always enough to scatter my thoughts.

I handed her a beer and then proceeded to spread out the blankets as best I could. The grass was damp, but the moisture did not seem to be a problem. I motioned for her to sit down before doing the same. The combination of blanket and thick grass turned out to be quite comfortable.

I took a sip of my beer while trying to think of something to say. We had spent a good deal of time together, but we both still fought youthful inexperience. I looked at her and let my eyes drink her in deeply.

The moon, apparently in tune with the two of us, shyly showed just a portion of itself. The lack of moonlight somehow enhanced the radiance of the stars. That starlight shined in her eyes, those incredibly light sapphire eyes, which made her seem extraordinarily alive.

I knew then what to say and I never spoke anything more truly. "You look so beautiful tonight. The starlight does something to you."

If it were possible, her eyes shined even brighter. The tiny dimple made an appearance. "Thank you."

She lowered her eyes and took my hand. Her thumb slowly traced the curve of it. When she looked back into my eyes, I saw something that had never been there before. Without knowing how, I knew it was love. It was also in that moment that I realized something, too. I loved her, as well.

The beer bottle in my other hand had suddenly become an annoyance, so I chugged the remaining Rocky Mountain brew, and tossed the empty aside. Kara could never do something as crude as chug a beer. She took a dainty sip and set hers on the blanket.

Even though we were alone, the night was full of sound. A chorus of frogs serenaded us from the far reaches of the pond. Crickets thrummed to their own tune. An occasional fish would splash the surface in search of food. A slight breeze rustled the leaves in the tree above us. She was right. It *was* perfect.

We settled down on the blankets. Kara rested her head on my chest. I could smell the scented shampoo she used in her hair. It mixed with her perfume to make a heady bouquet that intoxicated me in a way that the beer never could.

She sighed, then whispered in a quiet voice. "This is nice."

She could not see my face, but I smiled my agreement into her hair. "Yes, it is."

I tried to think of the right words. "Everything is as it should be," I whispered back. "The night. The breeze. The stars. You here with me."

She nodded her head in reply as she hugged me tighter. I was giddy to the point of delirium. I might not have known what I was doing, but it sure felt damn good.

I watched the stars for a while as we lay in silence. They were damnably bright. My thoughts escaped my lips. "Do you ever look at the stars and wonder if someone out there is looking down at us? You know, the same way we look up at them?"

She shook her head. "No, but it's a nice thought. Even if they were, I don't think it would be the same for them as it is for us."

"Why would that be?"

She rose up, and before I knew it, was sitting on top me. Her legs were to either side. Both of her hands pressed against my chest as she leaned forward until our noses touched. Her hair brushed the sides of my face.

"Because," she said, ever so softly, "they can't

love the way I love you."

We kissed, and something inside us broke. The tension, the knowing, and the desire for one another washed over us like a tidal wave. It was a torrent of white-hot flame that burned us and laid us bare before one another. There was no more hiding or holding it back.

On this night of bright stars and gentle breezes, we gave in to one another. We made love for the first time, our youthful awkwardness slowing us just a little. When I entered her, it felt as though the entire world had just righted itself. As if the universe had been imperfect until this moment.

It might have been an hour or a day. I really could not say how long we lay together. Time had no meaning for us. We both took what we needed. We gave freely with an urgent need to please.

We lay entwined together after we finished making love. The night air was cool on our sweating bodies. We both had crazy grins on our faces. My thoughts reflected on the feel of her soft body, the sensual curve of her breasts, and the amazing warmth between her legs. I wanted more of her. I wanted a lifetime of her.

Kara suddenly cried out. "Oh, shit!" She quickly

disentangled herself from me and hurriedly began pulling on her shirt.

I sat up and began to look around frantically. "What is it, Kara? What's wrong?" I could not see anything out of the ordinary.

She continued to get dressed. "It's after 1am. My parents are going to kill me!"

I did not laugh, but I wanted to. I was deliriously happy, which made it almost impossible to worry about anything at the moment. Still, I followed her lead and threw on my clothes. We quickly wrapped up the blankets, threw them in the trunk of the car and was soon on our way out of the park.

She did indeed get into trouble, but it did not matter much. We both knew that we had set ourselves on a path. It was a path we would walk together no matter what may come. Nothing in this world could separate us.

5

DECEMBER 18TH

Kara woke a couple hours later. I never moved from my seat. I wanted to be the first thing she saw when she opened her eyes. I took her hand and tried to sound cheerful. "Good sleep?"

She smiled the way that always reminded me of when she was seventeen. She squeezed my hand. "Yes. I feel a bit better now."

"Good. It's almost time for lunch. I hear there is meatloaf today!"

She shook her head. "No. You promised me a walk in the park."

It was tough to keep tears from my eyes. "But you love meatloaf. You should eat something to keep your strength up."

She chuckled. "Meatloaf is your favorite, not mine. I only put up with it because you like it so much."

I showed mock indignation. "I'm betrayed! You've been deceiving me all this time!"

"We women work in mysterious ways. Have you yet to learn that, my dearest?"

"I learned long ago to not delve too deeply into the feminine mysteries. I was always afraid that you would make a voodoo doll and cut off my balls."

She took in a deep breath. "You did not just say that!"

I let out a laugh then leaned in to kiss her. She placed a hand on my cheek to stop me. Our eyes locked, and once again I fought to not lose myself in those twin oceans of blue.

Her voice turned playful. "It was your silver tongue that you needed to worry about. As I recall, your balls worked just fine. Like they did that night in the park."

A broad smile split my face. "Ok, I get the hint." I reached over and pressed the call button that rested on her nightstand. "The mind is still willing, you know. I would jump your bones right now if I could.

Unfortunately, the only thing my balls are good for now is doctor examinations." I let out a sorrowful sigh.

Kara's smile turned to a worried frown. "Has it spread?"

I shrugged. "Not so much as before." I had brought up the subject, but I suddenly did not want to talk about it. I was saved by Nurse Ferrell sticking her head into the room.

"You called, Kara?"

I answered for her. "Yes, could you bring Kara's wheelchair? We're going to the park."

She applied the worried frown that all nurses seem to have. "I don't think it's a good idea. She isn't strong enough. It would take too much out of her. Not to mention that it's fifty degrees outside. I can't allow it. I'm sorry."

I looked at Kara before standing up and walking over to the nurse. I placed my hands on her shoulders and peered directly at her. "Nancy, we are going to the park." I then whispered, "For the last time."

Her eyes widened and I nodded. It shocked me to see the look of profound sadness that washed across her face. She whispered back, "I'm so sorry."

I patted her shoulders and stepped away. "We are ready to go now."

She gathered herself. "I'll be right back. I'll get your coat while I'm at it."

I moved back to Kara's bedside and returned my hand to hers. When she spoke, her voice was soft and full of emotion. "I wish you could."

I was puzzled. "What do you wish?"

"I wish that you could make love to me right now. I wish we could turn back time and go back in our youth to the park. Or the cabin." Tears began to roll down her face. "Take me there. Take me to the cabin."

The need in her voice nearly destroyed me. I reached down to gently wipe the tears from her cheeks.

It was at that moment Nurse Ferrell arrived with a wheelchair, along with another nurse for additional help. Kara was very fragile, so it usually took two people to get her into the chair. I took the time to collect myself while they worked. What could I say to her? Neither of us would be going back there. Not now.

The cabin. The memory of it is even clearer than

the one of the park. It was where our love was truly defined. It was a night that would leave its mark on our souls for the rest of our lives. It was the most precious night of my life.

6

THE CABIN

It was late. Very late. Time had slowed to a crawl. Each heartbeat in my chest seemed to last minutes. The sunset we had watched from the deck of the cabin earlier in the evening was now a distant memory. It seemed another lifetime ago. I began to wonder if this is what perfection felt like.

Kara was still in the bathroom doing whatever it is women do, so I took the opportunity to make a fire. This was a modern log cabin, and the builders had built in one heck of a fireplace. It sat atop pale white stones, which raised it several inches off the floor where lay an extremely thick rug. It was surrounded by large, smooth river stones that gave it the rustic look any cabin deserves. The mantelpiece was made of pure white marble. It held several frames that contained pictures of the owner's family.

After I had the fire to my satisfaction, I turned to look around the cabin. It was a basic one-room floor plan that assigned each section a certain task. The area near the fireplace was considered the living room. A small kitchen filled the far wall. In one corner stood a small table and chairs, while a queen-sized featherbed took up the other. The bathroom was the only room that had its own walls. It was quite the romantic retreat.

My favorite feature was the panoramic window that looked out over the back deck and across the small lake. I walked over to it and watched as the moonlight slowly played across the surface of the water. It, too, seemed stuck in time, as if the world was holding its breath.

My empty glass reminded me it was time for a new bottle of wine. I turned away from the window and made my way over to the kitchen pantry. I chose a bottle of red from the small selection and placed it on the kitchen counter. A previous lodger had thoughtfully hung a corkscrew from the refrigerator door. It took no time at all to have two fresh glasses poured and ready.

I glanced over at the bathroom door and wondered if I should consider a rescue mission. I shrugged. A call to the Coast Guard could wait a few more minutes.

I decided to help set the mood while I waited. I carefully carried the wine glasses across the room and set them below the fireplace. I then turned off the lights so that the flickering firelight was the only illumination. Satisfied at my handiwork, I sat down on the rug, and let the darkness settle over me.

The other side of the room was completely dark. The only visible light was emanating from around the bathroom door. Shadows danced as Kara moved across the light. I hoped that she was almost ready to come out and join me. I was not prepared for what I saw.

The bathroom door slowly opened to reveal a dream. Her body was silhouetted by the light behind her. It looked as though she were a dark shadow ringed with light. I could not make out her features, but I could see the feminine curves of her body. My eyes watched in fascination.

Kara placed one hand on her hip, the other on the wall. "Been waiting long?"

I did not answer. It was if she had taken the ability of speech away from me. I just continued to watch her as heat poured through my veins.

When she did not get an answer, she moved from the door with the most sensual walk I had ever seen. The firelight moved across her naked body as she came fully into view. The darkness behind her mixed with the orange-red light. It made her seem as though she were a goddess entering her lair. Never in my life, before or since, had I seen anything more beautiful.

She stepped onto the plush rug and lowered herself to her knees. It was then that I realized that I was not breathing. I was not sure if I was ever going to again. She gazed at me with those light sapphire eyes that blazed like two blue suns. I was completely transfixed. I knew in that moment time truly stood still.

She leaned forward and smiled at me. She was not wasting any time. "Nice fire. Now fuck me."

It was then that time resumed. My breath returned in a rush, and my heart pounded inside my chest with the force of hammer blows. I moved toward her as she fell into my arms. I did not think it was possible to kiss a woman as hard or as passionate as I kissed her in that moment. She returned my kiss with equal force as we lay each other down.

She gasped as I forcefully took her. She wrapped

herself around me as tightly as she could while I thrust deep inside. I felt pain as her fingers dug into my skin, but that only fueled my passion. Each downward thrust of my hips was a testimony to my lust that burned for her. I did as she commanded; I fucked her. We cried out in unison as the pleasure of our love overwhelmed us.

We did not stop. We made love every way we knew how and then invented new ways. We made our own song as the sound of the crackling fire mixed with our lovemaking. We gave each other everything we could give. Our souls entwined so that we were no longer two people.

I do not know how many times we both said, "I love you," but we meant it more each time. Our hearts grew, and from it blossomed a greater capacity to love. It was a beautiful thing to behold.

The first light of dawn spilled through the window to find us exhausted. We clung tightly to one another as if afraid the other would suddenly disappear. We had moved to the featherbed sometime in the night and were loath to leave it. The most magical night of our lives was coming to an end. I think we both felt the regret of that realization.

We drifted in and out of sleep for a couple more hours. We kept hoping to still find it dark outside when we woke. To our great disappointment, sunlight continued to shine through the window. It brought with it the unwanted day. We were not quite ready to dispel the magic we had created the previous night. Try as we might, we could not keep reality from knocking on our door. We reluctantly rose from the comfortable bed to begin preparations for the homeward trip. The two untouched wine glasses must have had quite a view.

We later learned that Kara was pregnant. The tragedy of our lives was not far behind.

7

THE ACCIDENT

"Help me." Kara reached out a gloved hand to take my own. I steadied her as best I could.

"Easy now. Take it slow."

The driveway was covered in ice. It had been difficult for me to make it to the car. It was even more treacherous for a sixth month pregnant Kara. It took a couple of minutes, but I soon had her safely inside the vehicle. I quickly jumped into the driver's seat and started the engine. Cold air blew in our faces as the unused heater struggled to warm the cabin. It was an agonizing wait.

The brutal winter had arrived early this year. It did not appear to be relenting any time soon. The news report stated the plows were experiencing difficulty keeping up with the snowfall.

Kevin Teague

Subsequently, the roads were in rough condition. I
was a little worried about that, but we had a
Thanksgiving dinner to get to. I let the car idle while
we waited for the heater to do its job.

The Thanksgiving holiday had snuck up on us
this year. It seemed like only yesterday that fall had
arrived, yet here we were freezing our butts off in
November. Christmas was not far behind. We had
barely started in on the preparations. Kara's focus on
the baby was singular and unwavering.

The air puffed in front of her face as she spoke.
"We better get going. Mom said they are all waiting
on us."

"Okey dokey." I put the car into reverse and
backed out of the drive. "Just tell her we are
practicing at being fashionably late."

Kara snorted a laugh. "Fashionably late doesn't
mean much around here, love. In fact, there's not
much fashion around here at all."

I glanced at her as I pulled out onto the road and
pointed the car towards town. "Did I just hear you
disparage your hometown? I don't think I have ever
heard you do that before."

She shook her head. "Some things are better left

unsaid. People around here are touchy about such things. We had better hurry."

"If you say so."

The quickly falling snowflakes were large and heavy with winter's promise. I turned the windshield wipers on in an attempt to help with visibility. The highway was already covered with a pristine white blanket that leeched away all color. It altered the landscape into a monochrome hue. I drove as fast as I dared.

Tall snow drifts filled the fallow cornfields that slid by on either side of the road. I had a crazy thought of stopping the car so I could run out into one of those fields to make a snow angel. I was able to restrain myself. Kara would not have been amused.

The waning glow of the sun painted the heavy clouds a pale orange. It was a pretty sight, but it also signaled the start of plunging temperatures. It was going to be a harsh night.

I noticed that Kara had wrapped her arms around her belly. "Is Kailey kicking again?"

Kara looked at me, her light sapphire eyes twinkling with joy. "Yes. She's getting stronger every day."

It had not taken us long to agree on a name after learning we were having a girl. A perfect name for what would surely be a perfect little baby. Kara was more than a little obsessed with the pregnancy. It was her greatest wish to have a child, and she went above and beyond to prepare for it. I sometimes thought she went too far with things, but I just chalked it up to being a mother's worry.

The tires slipped a little, so I let off the gas and made a small correction that allowed them to regain traction. The road really was treacherous. I would be glad to get to her mother's house. It was only a few miles away.

I reached out and took her hand. "She's going to be an amazing kid. Do you know how I know that?"

"No, how do you know?"

"Because Kailey has the best mother in the whole world."

She beamed at me. "Thank you."

Oh, how I loved to make her smile. "Now if we could only—"

It was then that the car lost traction and began to

slide sideways. I made a quick correction with my one hand, then yanked my other hand out of hers so that I could steer with both. The correction did not help. The car continued to slide down the road with the front of the car in one lane and the rear in the other.

Kara gasped, gripped my shoulder, and yelled, "Oh, my god!"

I corrected again. This time the front of the car began to swing in the right direction. I thought I had it saved until the wheels hit another patch of ice. The slick surface sent the car spinning out of control.

Kara screamed as we slid off the road and plunged down an embankment. I had a split second to see the tree before we hit. The passenger side slammed into it with a sickening crunch. I heard the shattering of glass as Kara's screams abruptly cut off. The ground fell steeply beyond the tree as we continued to slide down the slope. I frantically tried to stop the car, but our momentum was too great. The car flipped as it careened down the hill. My head smacked into something hard and unforgiving. Everything went black.

I regained consciousness to find my head resting on the steering wheel. The car had come to rest on its wheels. My head rang with the clangor of a thousand bells. My left leg burned like it was on fire. The air was bitter cold.

I groggily raised my head. "Kara?"

I looked over to see her slumped against the passenger door. The window glass had shattered. Her head hung limply on her chest. The howling wind was blowing snow into the car. Her face and shoulders were already covered with it. The snow was red with blood.

Panic filled me and I yelled. "Kara! Are you okay? Kara!" She did not answer. She did not move.

Pain cascaded down my body as I reached for her. It caused me to lose focus for a moment. I tried again and failed. The pain was excruciating. I attempted to see if she was breathing. The swirling snow made it impossible to tell.

"Kara! Wake up! Kara!" No response. I was scared to the depths of my soul.

I noticed her purse had somehow landed on the center console. I ignored the pain as best I could and reached inside to find her cell phone. My hands shook so badly it took me several attempts before I was able to dial 911. Darkness took me half way through the call.

8

DECEMBER 18TH

The park was across the street from Harrison Manor. It was not the park we had spent time at in the past, but it would do well enough. I shuffled alongside as Nurse Nancy Ferrell pushed Kara's wheelchair across the intersection and through the entrance to the park.

It was a beautiful day. The sun was high and bright. A scattering of cumulus clouds floated lazily in the pale blue sky. Nancy had been right. It did feel like it was fifty degrees. I zipped my jacket all the way up.

I turned to Kara. "It's beautiful out, if a bit cold. You couldn't have picked a better December day." A memory came to me. "It reminds me of my 50th birthday."

Her voice was weak when she answered. "Yes. A perfect day for it."

I let that one drop because we both knew what she really meant. I could also tell that she was already tiring from this brief foray outside the Manor. I wondered how long she would last. Thinking about it sent an icy chill through my chest that had nothing to do with the temperature. I pushed those thoughts aside and gazed across the park.

The park was small, maybe a quarter the size of the one back home. It was densely populated with oak and dogwood trees. Benches had been thoughtfully placed throughout where the best shade could be found. A walking path wound around a tiny pond near the center. I motioned for Nancy to take us in that direction.

We did not speak as we slowly made our way to the pond. We were both lost in distant memories. Memories of love and memories of deepest pain. It had taken us a lifetime to work through the worst of them. Now here we were, at the end of our lives, as deeply in love as we had ever been. Time had healed our terrible wound.

My old bones were aching something fierce. I turned to the nurse as we approached a bench. "Let's stop here for a bit. I need a rest."

She parked the wheelchair at the end of the bench and I sat down next to it. I let out a thankful sigh.

Nancy turned to me and pointed at the pond. "I'm going to take a stroll down there. You two rest here for a while."

I nodded my thanks as she turned and walked away. I then took Kara's hand and asked, "Are you doing okay?"

Her face was pale and her voice trembled when she spoke. "I'm doing okay. I just need to rest a bit."

We both knew it was a lie, but we also knew there was no going back. Her destination was in sight.

I gestured toward the pond. "That pond is not as nice as the one back home. It sure does bring back some great memories, though."

She smiled. "Some of the best. We did pretty well for our first time, didn't we?"

"Pretty well? I thought it was amazing!"

"It was, but compare that night with the one at the cabin."

She had a point. "Okay, but we had plenty of

practice by then."

She leaned her head back. "Mmmm, we certainly had." Her mind shifted locations. "Do you remember how mad my parents were after we got back so late from the park? I thought that I was going to get grounded for a year!"

I laughed. "I knew they wouldn't do that. Your parents liked me too much."

We both suddenly fell silent. We sat there for a long moment, each of us thinking the same thing. Yet another sad memory from our past that I did not want to remember. I distracted myself by watching a squirrel run across the brown December grass. It had a large acorn in its mouth. I imagined that it had dug it up for some additional nourishment to help make it through to spring. It raced up to an extraordinarily large oak tree and was soon out of sight amongst the dark branches.

It was Kara who spoke first. "It broke their hearts. After the accident, I mean. They thought I had become a crazy woman. It took me a long time to realize they were right."

"Kara, you don't need to say this. We have already been through this and put it behind us. Why bring it up now?"

Tears welled up in her eyes. I could see the sky reflected in them, blue on blue. "I must, my love. This is the last time. I need you to understand that it was all my fault."

"No, Kara. It happened and we can't change it. All we can do is be thankful for the time we've had together. It has been precious to me." I playfully touched her nose with my index finger. "Now who's the one thinking about bad memories?" Her smile was a half-hearted one. I counted that a victory.

She was dredging up memories from the murky depths of my mind. I had locked them safely away, but now the pain of those days was rising to the surface. So much pain. Raw, terrible pain...

9

LOSS

The first thing I saw when I opened my eyes was a ceiling that consisted of plain white panels. They surrounded fluorescent lights that provided a glow that seemed way too bright. I had to squint in order to see clearly. I could hear a beeping sound not far to my right. The soft hum of a machine came from my left.

The second thing I noticed was that I was in a hospital bed. Someone had pulled the covers up to my chin. Various tubes and wires appeared from all sides and disappeared under the blankets. I turned to my right to see an electrocardiogram machine counting off the beats of my heart like a crazy composer. A table stood behind it. Its surface was covered with flowers and greeting cards.

I was trying to remember why I was here when

Kara's mother entered the room. Sandra was much taller than her daughter, yet it was easy to see where Kara's facial features came from. Her mother had the same dimple on her chin. She stopped when she saw me. A strange emotion played on her face before she could hide it. She recovered and quickly put on a smile. She stepped up to the bed and pressed the nurse call button.

"You're finally awake! We were so worried about you. How do you feel?"

My mind did not seem to be working properly, but I managed to slur out a response. "What happened? Why am I here?"

She reached under the blanket and patted my arm. "You can worry about that later. Are you in pain?"

I tried to answer her question, but I was in such a fog that I could not seem to gather my thoughts. All I could say was, "I don't know."

"Well, you rest easy. I've called the doctor. He will be here soon to check on you."

I tried to nod my head, but all that did was cause the fog to thicken. I could feel my consciousness slipping away. I fought feebly to stay awake, but there was nothing I could do to stop it. I returned to the darkness a moment later.

I awoke sometime later to once again find Sandra at my bedside. A man in white clothing stood beside her.

The man spoke first. "Hello! I am Doctor Stephen Cord. Can you tell me how you feel?" He appeared to be in his mid-sixties. A wide paunch stretched tight his shirt, while wisps of silver hair valiantly tried to cover his balding head. His face was dominated by thick glasses that made his eyes appear bigger than they really were.

The fog in my mind was gone. It made it much easier to think clearly. It was as I regarded him that the memory of the car crash flooded into my mind. "Oh, no!" I tried to get up. "Kara! Where is she?"

The doctor pushed me back down. "Easy, son. You're not ready to be moving around just yet. You've been severely injured."

That scared me even more. I turned to Sandra. "Where's Kara? Is she okay? Please, God, tell me she's okay!"

She gripped my shoulder. "She's doing fine.

They have her in another room. She got badly knocked around but she will be okay."

I eased back onto my pillow. "Thank you, Jesus."

"Yes." Her voice sounded strange. The doctor interrupted before I could inquire as to why.

"You were both severely injured, but I think it likely that you will have a full recovery." His eyes darted to Sandra before quickly moving back to me. Something was not right.

I opened my mouth to ask, but again the doctor interrupted. "You had a severe head trauma and your left leg was broken in three places. We kept you sedated until we could verify that there was no greater injury to the head or brain."

"How long was I out?"

It was Sandra's turn to answer. "Four days."

My eyes widened in shock. "Four days? How is that possible?"

Once again their eyes flicked to each other before Sandra spoke. "It was a bad accident. The police said that you spun out of control and hit a tree. The car flipped on its way down the hill. It took them a long time to find you. You're both very lucky to be alive."

Images of the crash appeared before my eyes. "It was the ice on the road."

"Yes, so they said."

The doctor leaned over me and began checking my eyes with a tiny flashlight. "You're still on heavy pain medication. I need to know if you feel any discomfort. How does your head feel? Any blurry vision?

"Truth be told, Doc, I don't feel much of anything. My vision seems fine. Is my leg going to be okay?" It was then that I noticed for the first time that my leg was encased in a large cast.

"It will take some time, but it should be like new when we take off the cast."

I let out a breath. "That's a relief. When can I see Kara?"

The doctor straightened and annoyingly glanced at Sandra again. He began making his way toward the door. "I'll be back to check on you later." He was gone before I could say anything else.

"Sandra, what the hell is going on? Why isn't Kara in here with me? Is she really okay?"

She pulled over a chair and sat next to the bed. She then reached over to hold my hand in both of hers. "Kara will be just fine, but there's something you need to know."

I saw tears in her eyes. She was really worrying me. "What's wrong?" She did not answer. "Sandra, tell me. What is it?"

Her grip on my hand turned fierce. "Kara will be fine." Her hands began to shake. "She lost the baby." She began to sob. "I'm so sorry."

The words did not make any sense. "What?"

She wiped her eyes on her sleeve and steadied herself with a deep breath. "She lost the baby. The doctors said it was the impact from the tree that did it. They tried so hard, but they couldn't save her."

Lightning struck my heart. What she said was impossible. It had to be.

"No, that can't be. You're mistaken. You said yourself that Kara is fine."

"Oh, my dearest, I wish that were true. Kara *is* fine, but the internal trauma was too great. They couldn't save Kailey. She's gone. My little granddaughter is gone."

My mind refused to work. A cold numbness began to flow through my body. I looked at her and saw the tears and the stricken look on her face. Was it really true?

I do not know how I got the words out. "Kailey is dead?"

"Yes."

I let the truth wash over me. It scoured my flesh and burned my soul. "Kailey." I buried my head into my pillow and let the grief overtake me.

I do not know how long I was lost to the world. Sandra stayed with me the entire time. She held me, consoled me, and did everything she could to ease my pain. She had always watched over me. She proved it once again.

When I was finally able to surface from my grief, she hugged me, and kissed my forehead. "Can I get you anything?"

"I want to see Kara." I wanted to hold her, kiss her, and grieve with her.

She lowered her head and stared at her hands in her lap. "She doesn't want to see you right now."

Her words made no sense for the second time

that day. "What do you mean?"

She looked up at me. "Kara is overcome with grief. She isn't thinking clearly right now."

"All the more reason for me to be with her."

She shook her head "Not right now."

"Why not?"

I will never forget the look on her face when she said the words that broke my heart. "She blames you for Kailey's death."

10

BURIED LOVE

A week passed before I was allowed out of my hospital bed. It left me with more time to think about things than I wanted. The pronouncement that Kara's mother made to me earlier in the week still shook me to the very core of my soul. Those words still echoed in my head like a thunderclap.

'She blames you for Kailey's death.'

For her part, Sandra did not agree with her daughter. I will be forever grateful to her for that. She explained that Kara was quite literally out of her mind with grief and sense of loss. In desperation, Kara was looking for anyone to lash out at in order to make them feel what she was feeling. I was the natural target because I was the one driving the car.

I had a week to lay on my back and do nothing

but replay the accident in my mind over and over again. I would watch as my brain showed me the car traveling along the icy, snow covered road. I concentrated hard, but I never could see the patch of ice that sent the vehicle out of control. It must have been 'black ice.' Black ice is transparent and nearly impossible to detect. All you see is the roadway beneath it instead of the slick surface itself.

I tried so hard to think of what I might have done differently. What if I had corrected the wheel a different way? Would turning it less have been enough to change the outcome? Maybe turning it more would have brought the car around faster. If so, it could have allowed us to miss the second patch of ice. Maybe. Maybe not. It was agonizing and ultimately self-defeating.

That was not the worst thing I had to think about. I also had to come to terms with the fact that my daughter would never be born. I had not been able to do that yet. The soul-crushing despair often left me staring at the wall in numb surrender, leaving me unable to feel anything. I preferred it that way. The numbness would hold at bay the tears and complete heartbreak.

Then there was Kara. She still refused to see or talk to me. Her mother told me that Kara's body had healed nicely. Unfortunately, her state of mind had worsened. She would scream at anyone who mentioned mine or Kailey's name. Her father told me of times when she would start throwing objects around her room. She would smash anything she could get her hands on, while saying things that you could never believe would come out of her mouth.

We were all very worried about her. The doctor wanted her to see a psychiatrist. It was obvious that the mental trauma of losing our child had overwhelmed her ability to cope with it. She needed help to work her way through it. That should have been my job, but I was completely cut off from her.

It was now the day before I was going to be released from the hospital. I did not care what anyone said. I was not going anywhere until I saw Kara.

The door opened and Sandra entered the room. She was holding a couple of tall latte cups in her hands. Bless that woman. I am sure she brought them because she knew that it is one of my favorites. Even small things can help soothe a hurting heart.

I thanked her as she handed me one of the calorie-laden drinks. I took a sip before speaking. "Thank you, Sandra. It's delicious." I smiled my appreciation.

"Anything for you, dear. You get released tomorrow. Your Aunt Lisa will be here to pick you up. Are you ready to go home?"

My smile faded. "No, I don't have a home without Kara."

She shook her head. "That's not—"

I interrupted her. "I'm going to visit her today, Sandra. God himself won't be able to stop me."

She gave me a hard look. "I know you want to see her. I understand how difficult it has been on you—"

"No, you don't, Sandra. I'm sorry, but you can't know. The woman I love was severely injured. We lost our baby. You can't keep her from me. It's bullshit and it's cruel. I won't stand for it anymore. I will see her. Today."

"If you do, it will only make things worse for the both of you."

"How can you know that, Sandra? Maybe seeing me is the one thing she needs the most."

She set her coffee down and leaned in so that she was very close to me. "I'll put it to you blunt and honest. Kara has a sick mind right now. She is lost.

Her coping mechanisms have failed. It may take a long time for her to come back to us. The doctor said it is uncommon, but it can happen to women that go through trauma like this. Having you barge into her room will cause more problems than it solves."

I suddenly realized that I was not the only one who was dealing with Kara's issues. She was the parent, after all. I softened my words. "This has to be difficult for you and David, too. I didn't mean for any of this to happen. I'm sorry."

"I know you are, dear. We know it's not your fault. It was an accident. You couldn't have done anything about it. All we can do now is be strong for each other."

"Thank you, Sandra, but I've made up my mind."

She appeared sad. "I've explained the situation to you. Now you must do what you feel is right."

We spent the next hour discussing how we should handle my visit. In the end, we agreed that Sandra would go into Kara's room first to try and make the transition to me as smooth as possible. She still disagreed with my decision, but now that it was made, she would support me as best she could. It was a beautiful thing for her to do.

We took the elevator down to the first floor and took a right when the doors opened. Her room was at the end of a long hallway. The going was slow due to my inexperience with crutches. I counted down the numbers until we reached room 155. I stopped at the door and let Sandra slip into the room.

She opened the door a short time later and motioned for me to enter. I paused a moment to brace myself for what I might see. In what state would I find the love of my life? I stepped into the room.

A surreal scene played out before me. Kara was looking down at her mother from where she stood on the bed. She held a pillow in one hand and a drinking glass in the other. Her once beautiful light brown hair stuck out in all directions. It was dirty and full of tangles. Her hospital gown was torn and hanging loose around her.

That was bad enough, but it was her face that nearly brought me low. Her look of grief was so profound that it hit me like a physical blow. It was if I had just been shot. Her wild eyes were slightly unfocused.

We each stood there and stared at one another for a long second. Her eyes widened as she recognized me. Her mouth fell open. I thought that I had better say something. Anything. "Kara, it's me. How are you?"

Her arm moved as she threw the pillow at me. She screamed in a shrill voice. "Get out!" I barely had time to dodge the pillow before the drinking glass flashed past my head to smash against the wall behind me. She screamed again. 'You killed my baby! I hate you! Get out! Get out!"

I was frozen in place. I did not know what to do. Her mother tried to calm her down, but Kara fought her off. She jumped off the bed and came at me in a rush. Her fists began hammering my head and chest. "Get out! You killed her! You killed her!" I was horrified.

Sandra pulled Kara away and pushed me out of the room. "For god's sake, don't come back in here!" She slammed the door in my face.

My mind reeled and the world shifted. A crutch slipped as I tried to move down the hallway. The pain of my shoulder slamming against the wall sent waves of dizziness through my mind. I wildly swung my arms in a futile attempt to gain balance. I fell to the ground in a clatter of metal, plaster, and flesh. I did not try to get up. I sat against the wall and cried my soul out onto the clean white floor.

We met with a psychologist later in the afternoon. The doctor had been observing Kara for the past few days and was now ready to give us an evaluation of her condition. I was hopeful that we might finally get some answers as to what was happening to her.

I was accompanied by Kara's parents, Sandra and David. I immediately noticed the desk as we stepped into Doctor Michael Anderson's office. The wood had been covered in a dark stain until it was almost black. The part I found most interesting was the absolute neatness of it. A pad of paper and a pen lined up perfectly parallel to the edge of the desk. A black writing mat covered the exact center. A couple of fancy paperweights occupied the front corners. There was nothing else on it.

Doctor Anderson greeted us with a shake of the hand. He then motioned for us to sit in the plush leather seats that surrounded the front of his desk. He then opened a drawer and pulled out a folder that had Kara's name on it. He flipped it open without looking at it.

"Thank you for coming by today. I'm sure you're eager to know what I have learned about your daughter. I will get right to it. I have observed her for the past week. That observation, along with the few times she would speak with me, has given me a very good idea as to her condition. My colleagues and I concur that she has a severe form of PTSD." He considered us. "Do you understand what PTSD is?

The three of us exchanged looks before I answered. "It's called Post-Traumatic Stress Disorder, right? I thought it was something soldiers suffered with during war."

The doctor regarded us with sympathetic eyes. "That's what it is called, but PTSD can have many causes and take many forms. You don't need to be a soldier to experience extreme mental trauma, which is exactly what has happened to Kara."

David leaned in closer to the desk. "So you think that she has this PTSD thing?"

The doctor nodded. "Yes, we do. The physical trauma has combined with the mental to put her in a confused state of mind that doesn't allow her to accept reality. I will try to explain as best I can."

He grabbed the pen from the desk and leaned back in his chair. "The major symptoms of PTSD are generally classified under three categories. They are hyper-arousal, intrusion, and constriction. The terms may not mean much to the average person, but the definitions are what we are concerned about here."

He rested his elbows on the arms of his chair and placed an end of the pen in each hand. "Hyper-arousal usually includes exaggerated startle responses, anxiety attacks, outbursts of anger or rage, aggressive behavior, or physiological reactions to things that resemble an aspect of the traumatic experience. Kara has been exhibiting several of these indicators."

He continued. "Intrusion can include recurrent thoughts about the experience, flashbacks, nightmares, and anniversary reactions that coincide with the event."

He flipped the pen into his right hand. "Constriction can be referred to as the numbing of emotions. It is avoidance behavior where they try to avoid people, places, or things that might bring up bad feelings about the event." He focused on me. "As you know, she refuses to see you. That is a sure sign of it."

Sandra sighed. "This is all very confusing. What is it that we need to do to make her well again?"

The doctor took all of us in with his gaze. "This will be a long process. She will most likely need months, if not years, of trauma-focused cognitive-behavioral therapy. There are medications that can help with the process. In addition to that, we recommend a strong family-focused therapy which helps loved ones understand what she is going through."

Sandra reached into her purse and pulled out a tissue. She used it to dab her eyes. "I'm overwhelmed. What is the likelihood of a full recovery?"

"We can never know with situations like these. Some make great strides right away while others take months or years. You must prepare for the possibility that she might live with symptoms of this for the rest of her life."

Sandra leaned against her husband and began to cry. The doctor got up, walked around the desk, and came to kneel beside her. "Let's not get too worried just yet. There are great treatment plans available today. I'm sure we will find one that best suits what Kara needs."

She gave him a slight smile. "Thank you."

I had to ask the question that worried me the most. "What about me? I want to do everything I can to help her with this. How can I do that if I'm not allowed near her?"

He stood up and sat on the front edge of his desk. "I'm sorry, but we need to start her on the recovery process. I would recommend staying away for now. Unfortunately, you are the prominent trigger that sets off her negative responses. We need to get her mind moving in a new direction. I know this is tough for you to hear, but you must be patient for now."

It was the last thing I wanted to hear, but if helping Kara meant keeping my distance for a while, then I would do as they ask. Even so, it wounded my heart.

I went home the next day. I entered our house and wandered through each room. I could not help but notice all the loving touches that Kara had added to them. The living room curtains she had spent months looking for. The kitchen table she found while we were out antiquing. The king-sized bed that she just could not do without. I could not help but smile when I thought of all the love we had made in it.

The worst was the nursery. We had finished painting it right before the Thanksgiving holiday. The pink walls were pristine and untouched. The white crib sat forlornly against the wall. It seemed so lonely. Another round of tears filled my eyes. It seemed like the only thing I have done lately is cry.

I eased away from the crib until my back came up against the wall behind me. I slowly slid down it until I sat on the floor. The back of my head rested against the wall. I felt so many different emotions. They relentlessly warred against one another. It created a toxic mix inside me that continually filled me with sickening despair.

What I felt most was anger. Anger that this had happened to us. Anger that Kailey was gone. Anger that this was taking Kara away from me. Anger at feeling so damn helpless.

I did not know what I was going to do. I had no idea how I could help Kara. The scene in her hospital room scared me more than I cared to admit. What if she does not get better? How would I handle it?

I sat in Kailey's room for several hours trying to think of ways to help her. In the end, I did not come away with much. I would need to listen to the doctors and follow their lead. I prayed that they knew what they were doing.

Kara came home five months later. She seemed to have made good progress in her recovery, but she still had a long way to go. Countless hours of therapy and other programs had helped her come to an uneasy peace with the fact that Kailey was gone. I could be with her without any issue, but it was clear she tolerated my presence with unease.

I made sure the nursery had been repainted. I also had the crib and other baby items removed from the house. We did not want to take any chances at triggering a bad response.

We tried to get our lives back to normal, but I could tell there was something missing from her heart. She had not shown me any affection since the accident. She did not allow me to sleep in the same bed. We never held hands, which was something we always loved to do. It might have been the middle of summer, but our house was a cold one.

The year was slipping into September when the final blow came. We were in the living room. She was laying on the couch. I was sitting in my recliner. She used the remote control to turn off the show she was watching before turning to look at me.

"I'm moving back to my parent's house."

It came so out of the blue that I was not prepared for it. The magazine I was reading fell from my fingers. "What do you mean?"

"I don't love you anymore." She said it in such a matter of fact tone that she might as well have slapped my face.

My mouth worked but it took a while for words to come out. "You don't mean that. Of course you love me, same as I love you."

She stood up. "You took Kailey away from me. I'll never forgive you for that." She walked past me and headed for the bedroom. She apparently had farther to go in her recovery than we had assumed.

"Kara, stop." She paused at the bedroom door without turning around. "I love you. You've been making great progress. We just need more time."

She spoke without looking at me. "Will more time bring Kailey back?"

I sighed. "You know it can't. We can always try to have another child."

"No." She continued on into the bedroom.

I jumped out of my chair and went after her. I was not going to let this happen. I had already lost a child. I was not going to lose the woman I love. I entered the room to find her removing clothes from our closet. "Kara, you're not doing this."

She continued to throw clothes onto the bed. Her words cut like a knife. "Didn't you hear me? I don't love you. All you do is remind me of Kailey. I'm leaving."

I had been so patient with her this past year. I had put my feelings aside to make sure she had the time and help that she needed to get better. These events had taken their toll on me, both physically and mentally. I kept my pain hidden from view as best I could.

Kara needed help to get through the trauma of losing our child. What nobody stopped to consider was that I needed help, too. I hurt inside so much. I needed her support as much as she needed mine. She seemed unable to give it.

I grew angry as my head filled with these thoughts. I had given her everything my heart could give. It was time to take something in return. "What about me, huh? Have you stopped to think about what I've been going through? Do you think that you're the only one who hurts? I remind you of Kailey, do I? Well, that's how it's supposed to be. We're not supposed to forget her. We should cherish the time she was with us, even if she never left the womb."

The heat of my anger was growing to a fevered

pitch. It all came out in a rush. Everything I had held inside for so long came pouring out to land between us. "How dare you make this all about you? You've had it tough, tougher than the rest of us, and I'm sorry for that. What you need to realize is that you're not going through this alone. I'm here. I hurt the way you hurt. I cherish you because you do remind me of our child. Don't throw us away because life got hard. We need to support each other every way we can. It's the only way we can get through this."

Kara knelt down and pulled out a suitcase from underneath the bed. She began throwing the clothes into it. It was if she had not heard a word I said. "I don't want you in here. Leave me alone."

The knife dug deeper into my heart. "Kara, I know that you love me. You have it buried so deep inside that you can't find it right now. All you need to do is look for it. Don't push me away."

She did not say anything. My anger boiled again. I reached down and pulled the suitcase away from her.

I did not see it coming. She slapped me across the face as hard as she could. The unexpected blow knocked me back a couple of steps. My cheek burned as if it were on fire. I blinked away tears of pain to see her storming into the bathroom. The door slammed shut behind her.

She left the next day. Not a single word was spoken as she pulled her suitcase across the living room floor and toward the front door. What hurt the most was that she never looked at me as she reached the door and opened it. It was if I did not exist in her world anymore.

I let her go. She was not my Kara. The Kara I knew would never have done what she did yesterday. Her road to recovery stretched out before her to an unseen horizon. She had chosen to walk that road without me.

The suitcase bumped over the threshold as the door began to swing closed. I reached out a hand to her that she never saw. The click of the lock brought me to my knees. I bowed my head to grieve for the love we once shared.

Sandra called me later that year to tell me Thanksgiving had not been kind to Kara. The anniversary symptom of PTSD had reared its ugly head. At her doctor's request, they were admitting her back into the hospital. I had to finally force myself into thinking that we might never be a true couple again.

It was a fine spring morning when her mother came to see me. It had rained as the sun rose, but now the warmth of the day was drying the grass and forcing the small puddles to retreat. It would have been a very nice day.

We sat on the front porch and talked about the weather for a while. Eventually, Sandra brought up the reason for her visit. "I'm here because I love you like a son. I know that you love my daughter with all your heart. I have always been grateful it was you that she found. I believe she still has love for you in her heart. It may take a very long time for her to find it again. I don't know what form it would take if she did find it."

I nodded, but that was all I could give her.

She put her arm around my waist and pulled me close. "It is because I love you that I must tell you to start thinking about moving on with your life. Kara will not be whole for a long time. It's not fair for you to waste your life waiting for her."

I shook my head this time. "How can you expect me to give up on her? She is my love and my life. I can't walk away from her now."

"You can and you must. I don't know how long Kara's recovery will take. Nobody does. I want you to be happy again. You're not going to find happiness with Kara. Not for a long time, if at all."

I stood up and stepped off the porch. "This is nonsense, Sandra. I can't do it."

Her sad voice spoke a brutal truth. "She broke you heart when she moved out."

It was difficult to hide the painful sting I felt in my chest. "She wasn't herself. I still have hope that the Kara I love will come back to us. She has to. I'm lost without her."

She stood and hugged me. "I hope she does, too. I still want you to think about what I said. In time, you will understand."

Her last words echoed in my mind as her car backed away from the house. It was with a heavy heart that I watched her drive away.

11

DECEMBER 18TH

"Where were you?"

My head jerked up when I heard her voice. "What?"

"You were far away. Where did your thoughts go?"

"I'm not sure you want to know."

"Nonsense. Tell me."

I sighed and peered up at the sky. "I was remembering the days after you moved in with your parents. Your mother came to tell me that I needed to move on from you."

"Ah, I see." She sniffed. I glanced over at her to see her eyes shining wetly. "How long was it before you moved away?"

I lowered my gaze to stare at the ground. "I waited another six months. The doctors said you needed to begin integrating me back into your life. I tried numerous times to see you. You always refused. It broke my heart. Your rejection was too much for me to take. I had to get away."

Her small, frail body began to shake as the tears fell. Her voice was full of emotion. "How can you still love me after what I did to you?"

"Kara, I knew in my heart that you loved me. Your condition didn't allow you to see it. Yes, I was upset and hurt. It took years for me to understand my own feelings about what happened. I eventually came to the conclusion that I couldn't blame your heart for what your mind was doing to you."

I was worried she might hurt herself if she cried any harder. "You stayed away for so long. I never knew where you were. Why did you never come home?"

"You needed time to heal. Your mother called me a couple years after I left. She said you were doing much better and were attempting to begin your life again. We both agreed it would be best if I stayed away. My presence would have caused more harm than good. It was because I loved you that I stayed away. I wanted you whole again so that you could live a normal life. We spoke about this before, remember?"

She gave a small, wet laugh. "That was a long time ago."

I thought a moment. "Yes. Thirty-four years ago today, in fact."

12

GATHERING

"The party is about to start."

I studied my Aunt Lisa from where I sat on her couch. She was short and round with a long mane of black hair heavily streaked with gray. Her look was stern, which meant I was going to catch hell no matter what I did. My head was laid back and my feet propped up. I was comfortable and not yet ready to move. I was even feeling too lazy to speak, so I just grunted at her.

"Don't give me that, Mr. I-Want-A-Big-Gathering-With-Catered-Food-And-A-Band. This is your shindig. People will be arriving soon and you're the reason why. The least you can do is be there to greet them."

I switched from a grunt to a groan. She stepped

close and wagged a finger in my face. "And none of that, either. You'd better be out in the front yard in five minutes, or else! She turned and walked away. A minute later I could hear her banging around the kitchen. I smiled. It was good to be home.

It was my 50th birthday, but you would never know it to hear her speak. She and her husband Tom had taken over the job of raising me after my parents died when I was fourteen. She still thought of me as that troublesome teenager, even though I had been gone for more than twenty-five years. I loved her for it.

She was right. This was all my doing. I had been yearning for many years to visit family and old friends. They continually asked me to come home. The one overarching reason always kept me away. I could never bring myself to do it. The cost to my heart was too great.

I had moved to California in a desire to be as far away as possible. I found a job in the Petaluma area that made me happy, so that is where I began my new life. I made a good living. It allowed me to plan what I was doing now.

I was not about to stay away forever, so I hatched a plan to have a big birthday bash for myself. I decided to have it in my aunt's large back yard. She thought I was crazy for holding an outside birthday party in December. She came around when I told her that there would be a large tent with heaters to provide warmth. It would be just as comfortable as being inside her house.

So that is what I did. I hired a tent company to erect one of their largest pavilions in her backyard. It was big enough to hold several hundred people. I then had a stage erected for the band. Power was supplied from the house, while a large backup generator sat in readiness.

The caterer would supply ample amounts of barbeque ribs, steaks, and burgers along with plenty of side dishes and refreshments. I also made sure that we were amply supplied with varying types of alcoholic beverages. What could be more hilarious that watching drunk family and friends do funny things?

It was all easier said than done. My hope was that I could hire people to handle most of the large details. I should have known it would not work out that way. The placement of the tent was more difficult than anticipated due to its sheer size. Then there was the choosing of menu items. We had to make sure everyone's dietary needs were considered. Peanut allergies are a bitch to plan around.

Everyone had varying opinions on which band to use. While one person might like the Country Hills Band, another would say the singers sound like screeching cats and dogs. Twelve bands were considered and rejected before we had a majority vote for The Double Barrel Band. They would play various country and contemporary songs.

Almost all of these preparations fell squarely on my Aunt Lisa's shoulders. She would gather all the information as best she could. I would then get a call from her every night with the details. We would discuss it, and after some rather heated debates, finally agree on what should be done. She then had to organize and schedule everything while riding herd on people to make sure things got done. She was better at it than she would admit.

Everything took more time to get done than we thought it would. I suppose that was one reason why she was a little testy with me now. She completed most of the work before I arrived, and now that I was here, all she saw was me snoozing on the couch. I was not too worried. I had a plan to smooth her ruffled feathers.

I pulled myself up from the couch to the sound of various popping bones. This getting old stuff needed to stop. I was not quite ready for that downward spiral.

I grabbed my coat and stepped out onto the front porch. I was momentarily blinded by the bright sun soaring overhead. It was a beautiful December day. The high temperature was supposed to be around fifty-five degrees. The sky was clear of clouds and there was little to no breeze. So much for my aunt's weather worries.

I drank in the day as I put on my coat and breathed in the Midwestern air. The scent of open fields and dark earth filled me. It is a cliché, but it truly smelled like home. I suppose it was.

I glanced at my watch to see it was almost noon. The guests would be arriving soon. I was a little nervous. I had not seen any of these people for a very long time. I wondered how they would react to me after so long an absence. Would I know what to say to them?

I did not have to wait long to find out. The first car to arrive, a green Chevy Impala, belonged to Chris Brushard. He was an old high school buddy of mine. He got out of the car and came up to me with a smile on his face. He was just as thin as I remembered him, but his thick black hair had been replaced with a bald head. I reached out a hand, but he ignored it. He instead reached in to give me a hug.

"How you doing, ass wipe?"

I laughed. "Doing great, pizza face. Thanks for coming."

We both laughed. It was if we had gone back in time to when we busted on each other like this every day. It was a great feeling.

"Let me introduce you to my wife, Alissa."

"It's nice to meet you, Mrs. Brushard." She was pretty, with pale yellow hair and a nice figure.

"Likewise. Chris told me about all the trouble you boys used to get into. I don't think that I believe half of it." She smiled to let me know she was kidding.

"I'm not sure what he's told you, but whatever it was, it's all true."

Chris interjected, "Damn right!"

We all had a laugh and I slapped him on the shoulder. "The tent is around back. Feel free to eat and drink to your heart's content. The band will begin playing soon. I'll be along in a while." He took his wife's hand, which made me smile, and began leading her around to the back of the house.

Others began to arrive and I greeted them one by

one. I was pleased at how many had decided to come to my party. Quite a few friends and a smattering of family members were all soon helping themselves to the food and enjoying the band that was now in full swing. The music sounded good. We at least got that decision right.

I needed to get in the tent, being this was my own birthday party, but there was something I needed to do first. Despite her complaints, Aunt Lisa was flitting from house to tent and back in an attempt to make sure everyone was having a good time. I had no doubt that Tom was taking full advantage of the multiple kegs that were setup inside the tent.

She had just stepped out of the house with a big package of paper towels in her hands when I called her over. "Aunt Lisa, a moment if you would."

She gave me an exasperated look. "Can it wait? Someone knocked over the punch bowel and it's made a mess on the table."

I winced. "I just need a moment." I once again received that stern look. "Please."

She sighed before walking over to me. "What is this about?"

I beckoned her around to the front of the house in an attempt to gain some privacy. Once there, I hugged her and kissed her forehead. "I want to thank you for everything you've done for me. I don't mean just for the party, either. You and Tom stepped up and took care of me when others wouldn't. I don't have the words to express how much that means to me."

I pulled a small box from my coat pocket. "This is for you."

She glowered at me for a moment before accepting the gift. A small gasp escaped her lips when she saw what was inside. "It's beautiful!" She removed the necklace from the box and held it out for both of us to see. It was a golden owl inset with two large diamonds for eyes. "You shouldn't have done this."

"It's just a tiny payment for everything you've done for me. I could never hope to repay you in full." I took the necklace from her and placed it around her neck. "There you go. It looks fine on you."

She wiped away tears before giving me a big hug. "Thank you. You being here was enough, but this is very nice. I love you."

I had to fight off a couple tears myself. "I love you, too."

She smacked me on the chest. "Now get back in there and be with your friends. We will be bringing out the cake soon."

I smiled. "Yes, ma'am." Nodding, she turned and strode back toward the tent.

It was not long before I found myself thoroughly enjoying the day. I was in the tent and the party was going well. The band was playing some great songs, which had several people showing of their not-so-fantastic dance moves to the great entertainment of us all. The alcohol had been flowing freely and it most assuredly contributed to the frivolity. People were laughing and having a good time. I could not have asked for more. I felt genuinely happy for the first time in years.

The band was taking a break when I queued in line at what had become one of the most popular spots at the food table. The barbeque ribs were a real hit. A few minutes later I was standing with a full plate in one hand and a beer cup in the other. I was talking to another high school friend, Joe Huxley, when every conversation in the room fell silent. I looked up from my plate to see every eye locked on something behind me. I heard someone say, "Oh, no." Concerned, I turned around to see what was happening.

My eyes followed everyone's gaze to the back of the tent. A solitary figure stood in the entrance. Food and drink fell from my hands as I saw the ghost that had come to haunt me. Everyone around me faded away into mist. My world compressed into a hazy tunnel where no sound or thought existed. The haze began to swirl as the figure moved toward me. As it came near, twin orbs of blue burned a hole through my heart.

She rushed toward me and fell into my waiting arms. Our embrace was long and fierce. The voice was unmistakable, even after more than twenty-five years. It was muffled from her face being pressed into my neck, but I could clearly hear Kara whisper two of the most beautiful words I had ever heard.

"You're home."

I was still in shock thirty minutes later. Kara was sitting next to me with a quizzical look on her face. In a need for privacy, we had taken a couple chairs and moved from the tent to sit under a tree in the front yard. I was still trying to decide if I was dreaming.

She broke the silence with a laugh. "You should have seen your face. It was if someone had punched you!"

I blushed with embarrassment. I ducked my head before I replied. "I...I never thought that I would see you again. I thought you were lost to me forever."

She used a hand to gently pull up my chin. She shook her head at me. "Not forever."

My heart felt as though it were riding a roller coaster. "How did you find out I was here?"

She snorted a laugh. "It was impossible to not find out. You invited almost everyone from high school. Except me."

I felt as awkward as a teenager. I needed to steer the conversation in another direction. "You look beautiful." She did, too. I might have been biased, but with the exception of a few lines around her eyes, it seemed as though she could be half her age.

Her reply saddened me. "I don't feel beautiful."

The urge to reach out and touch her face was overwhelming. "You *are* beautiful. If my word means anything, then know it to be true."

She looked away. "I don't see it that way." She must have felt the need to change the subject, too. "Where have you been all these years? I suspected that my mother knew your whereabouts, but she never told me."

"I went to California."

"So far away. What did you do there?"

I thought of the many years that I had spent on the West Coast. The general mentality and lifestyle was so much different from the Midwest. "I tried to build a life. I got a job at a big aeronautics company. I've worked there for more than 20 years."

She rested an elbow on her leg and cupped her chin in one hand. "What did you do there?"

"Technical things, mostly. I run computer simulations to test stress tolerances on newly designed aircraft parts. It might sound boring, but I actually find it quite interesting. I get to see some neat things come down the assembly line."

"Wow!" She sounded genuinely impressed. "You must be some kind of smart rocket scientist!"

"I don't know about that!"

She smacked my knee and laughed. "I'm teasing! I always knew that you would be successful at whatever you decided to do."

I felt like blushing again. "Thank you."

Her playful tone turned serious. "I noticed you're not here with anyone. Did you never marry?"

"No."

"Why not?"

The answer to her question had so many complicated layers. I decided to be as straightforward as I could. "I had a few relationships. There were a couple of them that were meaningful enough to last a few years."

She surprised me with her next question. "What were their names?"

"You want to know their names? Why?"

"I just do."

I knew this had to be dangerous territory. "Sarah and Carol."

She asked another complicated question. "Why did you not marry one of them?"

I thought about my past and how my vision of the future never panned out. "I don't know. I suppose it's because there was always something that didn't feel right." I paused. "No, that's not the correct word. The best way to say it is there was never something that felt perfect. You see, I had already known perfection."

She abruptly stood and walked away from me. She reached the end of the yard and stopped at the edge of the road. I worriedly got up and followed her. I arrived at her side to see she had crossed her arms beneath her breasts. Her eyes were staring across the empty cornfields that stretched across the landscape.

We stood there without speaking. The desire to kiss her was overwhelming. I could tell that she had something more to say. I waited until she was ready to share it.

She turned to me with an unreadable face. "My first daughter is named Sarah. She recently turned nineteen."

I wondered when we would get around to this subject. I nodded my head in acknowledgment that I knew. "I heard that you had married. You have two other children, don't you?"

"Caitlyn is seventeen and John is fourteen."

"Nice names."

Her stare was intense. She spoke with an urgency in her voice. "You understand, don't you? So many years went by and I didn't know where you were. I needed someone. I needed someone to help me forget."

I placed an arm around her and pulled her close. "It's okay, Kara. I do understand. I was happy for you. It meant that you were moving on with your life. It gave me hope that you were close to a full recovery. Your happiness has always been my greatest concern."

"It didn't bother you?"

I thought about the emotions that went through me when Sandra told me that Kara was getting married. How do I explain the debilitating sense of loss I felt? Do I tell her of the sadness and depression that chased me for years? I could not do that to her.

"Of course it bothered me. The love of my life – my soul mate – was about to spend her life with another man." I really did not want to go down this road, so I took another. "What made me most happy was when you had a child. That proved to us all that you had fully recovered. I was very proud of you."

Her smile was a sad one. "We were married for many years before I was ready to try. I was so scared during the first pregnancy. Everyone was on pins and needles around me the entire time. I guess that I can't blame them."

I glanced back at the house. I noticed that not a single person had left the tent. That was odd, but I could not think about it now. "Everything went okay, didn't it?

A smile lit up her face. "It went great. I didn't have a single problem with her." I could hear the sound of deep relief in her voice. "It was like the weight of the world had been lifted off my heart when I saw that Sarah was safe and sound. It changed everything for me."

I was happy for her, but I felt nothing but sadness for myself. "Was it that success which motivated you to have more?"

"Yes, it did. I knew that I could have a child and not…" Her voice trailed off.

She did not need to say anything more. "I know."

I turned and wrapped my arms around her. She began to cry on my chest. "I'm so sorry. So Sorry.

So sorry." She kept repeating those two words.

I ran my fingers through her hair, then gently raised her head so that I could look in her eyes. I spoke in a quiet voice. "Hush now. Everything is okay. You're safe and your children are well. I suppose even I am safe." Something flashed in her eyes while I spoke. I was not sure what it was, but it seemed familiar.

The sound of voices brought my head up. I saw a few people coming from the back of the house. It seemed a few adventuresome souls decided to go on a scouting party. I could see them staring at us.

Kara regarded them with disdain. "Let's go for a walk."

My heart swelled when she took my hand. She pointed a direction and we started for the road. She could have been leading me to the Pits of Doom. It would not have mattered. I would have gone willingly and without complaint.

We were about a block away from the house before she spoke again. "I want you to know that I'm healed. Heart and soul. It took many years for me to escape from my grief." She stopped walking and stared down at the dark asphalt. We were standing in the shade provided by massive oak trees that overhung the road. "I lost Kailey. I lost you. It took years before I understood that neither loss was your fault. I said awful things to you. Terrible things."

"Kara." I tried to interrupt her. She interrupted me instead.

"No, hear me out. I considered a long time on what I would say to you if I ever saw you again. I need to tell you this."

I sighed, but acquiesced. "Okay. Go ahead."

She paused for a moment to collect her thoughts. "I was a different person after the accident. The mental pain was so great that it pushed the real me aside. It made another person. It was if I were outside myself and looking at a stranger who tried to hurt everyone around her. She focused all the blame and her hate on you."

Another pause as the tears came. "I tried to stop it. I screamed and clawed but I couldn't break through. I was lost inside myself. I was a prisoner inside my own mind. It took what seemed an eternity, but the doctor's helped me to climb my way out of that invisible cage. I began to think rationally again. I looked for you. They told me you were gone." More tears now.

I reached out to hug her again, but she pushed me away. "I'm not done. You need to know that I don't blame you for any of it. It was an accident and there's nothing you could have done to prevent it. I was the one who drove you away. I don't blame you for leaving after the way I treated you. I can't imagine how you must have felt toward me."

I decided to do some confessing of my own. "It hurt more than you could ever know. The doctor told us what was wrong, but it was still your voice saying those hateful things. I had to get away, for your sake, and for mine."

Her next words were a broken cry. "I broke your heart."

"Yes."

She ran into my arms. I let her cry on my shoulder as I slowly rocked her back and forth. I shared my tears with hers.

After our tears had abated, she looked up at me with her light sapphire eyes. I could no longer resist. I kissed her. My heart leapt with excitement when she returned it with one of her own.

The sound of an approaching car brought us out of our quiet moment. I recognized it as one that had been parked in the driveway. I could also see a couple more cars backing out onto the road.

"I guess they've decided that the party is over." I smiled down at her. "You're quite the party crasher."

She began wiping away her tears with the back of a hand. "I'm sorry. It was not my intention. I just had to see you. This was the only place I knew you would be."

I waived that away. "Don't worry about it. Having you here is the best birthday present I could ever hope to receive. Besides, I'm willing to bet the reason for the exodus is either the food or drink has run out."

More cars went past as we made our way back to the house. It really did look like an exodus. Another concern came to mind. "This will get back to your husband. Will this cause trouble for you?"

She shrugged. "I don't know. He knew I was going to see you today. He didn't like it, but I told him I was doing it no matter what he said."

"Let's hope he understands the situation."

She did not say anything as we reached the front yard. We sat in the chairs we had vacated earlier. I waved at a few of my guests that were getting ready to leave. Everyone seemed to be in a hurry. It seems a small town never forgets anything.

Kara paid them no mind. "Did you ever think about coming home?"

"All the time."

She smacked a fist on her leg in anger. "Mom wouldn't tell me where you were. I wanted you home, but she wouldn't tell me! How could the two of you make that kind of decision behind my back?"

I grabbed her fist before she used it again. "Do you think I wanted to leave? Do you know how many times I loaded up my car and started to drive back here? I tried to come home several times. I always found a reason to stop myself."

"Why? Why did you stop?"

I took in a deep breath of crisp December air. "For one simple reason. I love you."

Her voice had an edge to it. "How is that love?"

"Kara, loving you meant staying away so that you could get the help you needed. We had no idea what would happen if I returned. I could not take that chance. I was not going to cause you any more pain."

Her tone grew heated. "You don't love me. How can you love me after what I did to you? Admit it! You stayed away because you hate me!"

I still held on to her hand and I was not letting go until she understood how I really felt. "You're wrong, Kara. I have always loved you. I always will. Would I have kissed you back there if I hated you? Everything I have done is because of how I feel for you."

I was feeling a little heated myself. "You wanted me to understand some things. Well, now it's my turn to make you understand. There has never been a day gone by that I didn't think of you. There were reminders of you everywhere. Even if I was far away. There were times when I would be driving in my car and I'd hear one of our songs on the radio. More than once I had to pull off the road to collect myself. Other times, I would daydream and think about all the nights we made love. You never left my thoughts. You were always in my heart. Nothing will ever change that. I still love you and that's just the way it is." I let go of her hand.

We sat there and stared at one another. I think we both were afraid to be the next one to say something. She spoke first. "I had it in my mind all these years that you hated me. It was the only thing I could come up with to explain why you never came home."

I gave her what I hoped was my most reassuring smile. "I never hated you. You hurt me. I felt anger toward you, but never hate. I loved you too much for that."

She stood and stepped in front of me. Bending down, she placed a hand on each of the chair arms. She then leaned forward and kissed me. Her next words would echo in my heart for the rest of my life. "I still love you, too."

Aunt Lisa's voice was faint, but I could hear her from where she stood on the porch. "Well, shit."

13

TO LAST A LIFETIME

I sat in my hotel room with an intense impatience. It kept bouncing me around as though I were a ping pong ball. For the moment, I was situated in a cushioned chair that took up the space between the king bed and the large window. I pulled the curtain back to see the final rays of sunlight disappearing behind the horizon. I checked my watch to find it was six o'clock in the evening. It always annoyed me at how early it got dark during the winter months.

Kara and I had beaten a hasty retreat after Aunt Lisa found us in her front yard. She had taken me aside and berated me for several minutes about messing around with married women, even if the married one was Kara. I told her everything was all right and there was nothing to worry about. I was not sure if that was a lie or not. I promised her I would be back in the morning to help with the party cleanup. I left her standing on the porch with her hands on her hips.

Kara soon left, but not before it was decided that we would meet up again later in the evening. The only private place we could quickly come up with was my hotel room. We both pointedly avoided the implications of that location. We simply pretended it was a convenient place to meet. Now that I had a couple hours to think on it, I was still not quite sure what would happen.

She probably just wanted to talk some more. We did not have much catching up time at the party. I think we were both fighting through feelings and emotions we had not faced head-on in many years. There were things I needed to say to her. I hoped to get that chance tonight.

I stood up and turned from the window. My impatience was getting the better of my nerves. I began to pace my way back and forth around the room. I had just reached the door when a soft knock stopped me in my tracks. I took a couple deep breaths to calm myself before I reached out and opened the door.

Kara stood there in all her glory. Despite the cold weather, she was wearing a red summer dress that stopped short of her knees. High heels brought her closer to my height. I caught a glint in her light sapphire eyes that made my pulse quicken. She looked damn sexy.

I had not realized that I had been standing there like a mute until she decided to bring me out of it. I could hear the amusement in her voice. "Are you just going to stand there or can I come in?"

I shook myself to clear the spell she had placed on me, then turned to allow her into the room. As I followed her in, I could not help but notice she still had the sexy walk that made my skin tingle. I was beginning to worry if I would be able to control myself.

She made a trip around the room. Her eyes took in the bed, love seat, and chair that made up the majority of the furnishings. She nodded in approval. "This is a nice room." She reached up and closed the curtains.

I cleared my throat just to make sure I still knew how to make sound. "Thanks. I like to treat myself when I travel."

She frowned. "I don't get to travel much. The kids take up most of my time."

"I bet they do." I could not take my eyes off her. "You look stunning. You've still got it."

Her laugh tinkled throughout the room. "I'm not sure what 'it' is."

I reached out a hand. "I'm glad you're here."

She took it and stepped close. "Me, too."

My pulse quickened as I studied her. I had not seen her face for more than half my life. Pictures and daydreams were an inadequate substitute for the true beauty that now stood so enticingly close. My body ached with longing for her.

I looked into her cerulean eyes and was swept away to another time. A time before our lives changed forever. A time when there was nothing but love. I spoke in a whisper. "May I have this dance?"

She smiled and took my other hand. We stood close to each other as we began to slow dance around the room. There was no need for music. We danced to the music of our memories. They were more beautiful than any song could ever be.

Kara rested her head on my shoulder as we danced in small circles. The scent of her reminded me of our youth. The memory of the first time we made love came to me and filled me with delight. I wrapped my arms around her and pulled our bodies together.

She sighed in contentment. "Don't let go."

"Never."

We stopped our dance to continue holding each other in a tight embrace. I heard her breathing and was comforted by it. I was holding her in my arms and it was not a dream. It was real.

I heard the intake of her breath as I lightly kissed her neck. She turned her face up to me and I kissed her cheek. A small sound escaped her lips as our mouths met as one.

It was long minutes before we stepped back to see each of us smiling at the other. She took me by the hand and led me over to the bed. As we sat down, I wondered if I should put my arm around her.

It seemed as though she wanted to resume our earlier conversation. "Have you traveled to many places?"

I thought about the places I had been. It was not a terribly impressive list. "Oh, I've gone on a couple cruises. Hawaii is an amazing place. Las Vegas isn't all that far from California, so I go there every now and then to blow off some steam."

"I'd love to go to Hawaii someday. They say it's a beautiful place." She sounded wistful.

I nodded. "It is very beautiful. You should make your husband take you there sometime."

She gave a resigned sigh. "That will never happen."

"Why not?"

"It just won't. Was your Aunt Lisa mad?" I was getting used to the abrupt changes of subject.

I barked a laugh. "She's always mad about something. I was able to calm her down. She just worries about me, that's all."

She leaned against me and put her arm around my waist. "That's a nice thing to have. Someone who worries about you, I mean."

Feeling like I had just been given permission, I put my arm around her and squeezed. "Yes, it's nice to know somebody cares."

"I care." She turned her head to place her lips next to my ear. Her next words were a soft whisper. "I've gone without you all these many years. I want this night to be about us. No more talk about anyone else. It's just you and me tonight. Okay?"

I turned to look into the eyes that had stolen my heart so long ago. "Okay."

She reached up to place a hand on my cheek. "We have a lot of time to make up for."

She leaned in and kissed me before I could reply. My blood flash-boiled as I took hold of her and pressed my lips against hers. She moaned as our tongues urgently explored. It felt as though electricity was being fed into every nerve ending in my body. We were both out of breath when we pulled apart. "Wow," was all she could say. I nodded my head in complete agreement.

She stood up and took a couple steps away from the bed. My eyes were transfixed on her body as she turned to stand in front of me. Her eyes were twin flames of blue. "Do you see me?"

The room was darkening, but I could see everything about her. I could see the light brown hair that reached her shoulders. I could see how the red dress clung to her delicious curves. I could see her hard nipples straining against the inside of the fabric. "Yes."

She pulled at the shoulder of her dress and let it drop to the floor. She was naked. I could hear the need in her voice. As was her way, she did not waste any time. "Take me."

There was no fantasizing now. She had struck the match and I was on fire. My eyes drank in the beauty of her. Her still-firm breasts hung above a flat stomach that gave way to shapely hips and the soft curve of perfect thighs.

I reached for her and she stepped close to me. I kissed between her breasts, then moved to each nipple so that my tongue could have them. They were as hard as diamonds by the time I began to move downward. I slowly kissed her stomach as my mouth went lower.

Her breath quickened as I reached the small patch of hair between her legs. Her voice was breathless. "Oh god, yes. You're the only one to do this for me. Don't stop. Do it."

A flash of surprise went through me, but I quickly dismissed it. I grabbed her ass with both hands and pulled her onto my waiting lips. She gasped as my tongue began to explore her. She was soaking wet. A little "Oh!" escaped her as I flicked her clit that was as hard as I was.

I pulled back my head, lifted her up, and threw her down onto the bed. I then lowered myself to my knees. I pushed her legs apart, then used my fingers to open her. My tongue went to work once more.

The heat poured from her as she grabbed my hair in both hands and pressed my head down into her. The scent of her sent shivers down my spine. The taste intoxicated me. She made tiny little sounds with each flick of my tongue. My growing arousal was a dam that was about to break.

It was not long before her body began to shake. I felt the orgasm on my tongue as it washed over her. It was then that every thought vanished from my mind. I completely surrendered to my desire.

She was still in the final throes of her orgasm when I climbed onto the bed. I lifted her legs up and hooked an arm behind each knee. I leaned forward, which pressed her knees down toward her head, and raised her ass off the bed. A sharp cry escaped her as I entered her to the root with a hard thrust. Her wet embrace surrounded me in sensual waves that covered me in warmth.

I had made love to Kara and other women in the past, but this time was different. Some ancient animal instinct raised a passion inside me that I had never felt before. The years of absence had stoked a fire within me that was now a raging inferno. I took her not with just my body, but with my soul, as well.

I lowered myself until my head was just above hers. Our eyes locked as I worked in and out of her. Our hunger reflected in vivid blue and dark green. We breathed in each other's breath as our sex became more frantic, more needful. She bit my lip before lowering her head back in submission. I was in complete control of her body.

The feel of her skin against mine urged me onward. Each thrust brought a small "Uh!" from Kara, with each one coming quicker until we reached climax. She began to shake with another orgasm as I exploded inside her. We were both out of breath when we finally came back to ourselves.

I was finally able to pant out a "Fuck!" To which Kara's reply was, "No shit!" We had never been accused of being eloquent.

It was only then that I realized I had pulled her legs as far forward as they would go. It pleased me to see she was still so limber. Still, I eased up a bit, as I knew it had to be uncomfortable for her.

She raised her arms and wrapped them around my neck. "We've made love many times before, but what you just did was something different. It was primal." She grinned wickedly. "For a moment there I thought that I heard you growl."

I did not remember doing that. "Really? Well, as you said, we have a lot of time to make up for. It had been building up for more than twenty-five years."

She purred. "The way you just fucked me? I believe it." She pulled my face down toward hers and we kissed.

A little while later we lay in bed and spooned our bodies. She was in front of me. Her butt pressed into my crotch. I had one leg draped over hers, while my arm was wrapped around her waist. I was in Heaven.

Kara's voice sounded dreamy. "It was true. What I said earlier, I mean. My husband has never wanted to lick my pussy." She smiled mischievously. "I remember how you loved to do it."

I moved a hand to gently squeeze one of her nipples. "I still do. I love the taste of you. It's his loss." I dropped my hand from her breast to reach down and slide a finger inside her. She gasped a little as I pulled it out and brought it up to her mouth. I spread her juice on her lips, which she then slowly licked off with a careful tongue. "See what I mean?"

"Mmmm." She wiggled her butt against my crotch. I felt my blood begin to flow downward again.

I whispered in her ear. "How much time do we have left tonight?"

She glanced at the clock on the nightstand. It was getting late. "A little while yet." She wiggled her butt again. "Time enough."

That was all I needed to hear. I raised myself up and pressed her body face down on the bed. I was fully erect by the time I got between her legs.

Kara's voice was low and rough. "Hold me down."

We had done this in our past, so I knew exactly what she meant. I placed my hands on the back of her shoulders and pressed down as I slid myself inside her. I stretched my legs out behind me and braced myself on her shoulders. The magical rhythm began again. I could hear her wetness as I moved in and out of her.

Pressing down on her like this always turned me on, and she liked to feel my weight on her. Her head was turned to the side. I could see that her mouth was open but no sound escaped her lips. The primal urge filled me again with strength. My hips pressed against her ass with each thrust. Her hands reached above her head to grab a pillow in a forceful grip. I felt her join my motion as she raised her ass to meet each downward stroke. She allowed me to have my way with her again. I held on as long as I could, but I soon felt her walls begin to convulse. It drove each of us to yet another strong orgasm.

We lay together for a while, each of us taking turns to touch and caress. Kara's voice was one of contentment. "Not bad for an old man."

I softly kissed her cheek. "This old mule has a few miles left in him."

She laughed and rolled herself on top of me. Her hair hung to either side of her face, but I could still see her smile. "A mule is he?" She grabbed my cock and began to stroke it. "Is he a tame mule? Or does he need to be broken in?"

I did not think I had another time in me, but the sight of her body above me was enough to kick start the chemical reaction that rules all men.

She lowered herself onto me and began rocking her hips back and forth. I lifted my hands to cup her breasts. I used my thumbs to caress her nipples. She arched her back in pleasure as her hips ground into me with an ever-increasing pace. This time it was I who surrendered. We enjoyed this one for a long time before I began to feel the tidal wave rush through me once more.

She sensed I was close. She leaned forward to grab my arms and force them down to my sides. She rode me fast and hard. All I could hear was our heavy breathing mixed with the sound of our motion. She cried out when I came inside her. Her chest was heaving from the exertion as she lowered her head to mine. We kissed for a long, long time.

I watched her wince as she lowered the red dress down over her body. "Something hurt?"

Her smile was playful. "What do you think? I've never had my legs pulled up that far in my entire life. Were you literally trying to put my ankles behind my ears?"

I gave her a serious look. "Well...yeah."

She picked up a shoe and threw it at me. "Thanks a lot!"

We laughed and I stepped close to give her a kiss. I was trying to hide my fear of her leaving, but she must have caught something in my eyes. "What is it?"

I made a simple plea. "Stay with me."

She sat on the bed and slumped her shoulders. "I

want to, but I can't."

I sat down next to her and took her hand. "Yes, you can. I'm here. I want you to go away with me."

She glanced down at her feet. "I can't leave my family. My kids need me."

"What about me? I need you. Can you deny what happens to us when we're together? Can you forget the love we made tonight?"

She raised her head to look at me. "No, I can't deny it. I will never forget. I want for the rest of my life what we had tonight, but my family has become my life. I can't leave my kids. I can't put them through that. You must know what they mean to me."

I knew that I was losing her, but I had to keep fighting. "Do you love me?"

She placed a hand on either side of my face. Tears were filling her eyes. "Of course I love you. I always will. I will never love another man the way I love you. No man could ever satisfy me the way you do."

I placed my hands over hers. "Then come with me. Be with me. Let's make up for all the years we've lost."

She slowly shook her head. "I can't. I'm sorry. My life is too complicated for that now. You are free and can do as you wish. I have obligations to my children. I love them with all my heart. I won't cause them that kind of pain."

My tears were now flowing along with hers. "We were meant to be together."

"Yes."

"We are perfect together. Can you see that?"

She lowered her hands to her lap. "Yes, I see it."

My voice broke up a little when I spoke. "But you won't come with me?"

Her answer was devastatingly simple. "No." She turned her head away and quietly began to sob. I reached for her, but she stood up and began gathering up her shoes.

I wiped away my tears. "So tonight is supposed to last us a lifetime?"

She didn't look at me when she answered. "It will have to, even if this wasn't enough. It will never be enough." She paused. "Maybe this was a mistake."

I stood up and walked over to her. She kept her

back to me as I wrapped my arms around her. "This can't be the end. We just found each other again. I can't live the rest of my life without you. I need you."

Her tears intensified as she pulled away from me. "It's too late. I love you, but it's too late. Forgive me." She started for the door.

My heart panicked. This could not be happening. I was about to lose her all over again. I called out to her. "Kara, wait!" She stopped at the door to peer back at me. Her red dress was stained with tear drops.

I had to make one more plea. "I will be in town for a few more days. Maybe you'll change your mind. Maybe you'll see me again and change your mind. It could happen."

She stood in silence. We each regarded the other with tear-clouded eyes. She turned and opened the door.

"Kara."

She stopped in the doorway.

"I love you."

Her voice echoed the heartbreak I felt. "I love

you, too."

She stepped into the hallway and closed the door.

14

THE LAST APPEAL

The remainder of my birthday week was uneventful. Despite the tears and heartbreak of the previous night, I returned to Lisa's house to help with the cleanup. I did not have any words in me, so I worked in silence. I could tell that Lisa suspected something had happened between Kara and me, but out of respect for us, said nothing.

She told me the guests decided to leave early. They sensed we needed time alone. It seemed our history was more well-known than I would have imagined.

I spent the rest of the week roaming around town. I would drive around for hours with no particular destination in mind. I was lost and had no idea what I was trying to find. I felt empty inside, as if a large and important piece of myself had gone missing. I hoped that I would get another chance to fill the growing void within my heart.

I took the opportunity to visit the cemetery on my last day in town. I had been avoiding it all week. I realized that I had a difficult choice to make as I drove the car onto the gravel drive that made a loop through the memorial park. I decided to visit my parents first.

Their monument was well maintained. Flowers filled the marble vases that sat to either side of the stone. I knew Aunt Lisa stopped by every now and then to make sure it was kept up nice. It was another loving gesture that endeared her to me even more.

I contemplated my parents' names for a long while. I missed them so much. I wondered if they knew what was going on in my life. Would they be looking down on me with saddened eyes? Would mom be reaching her arms out to me while saying that everything would be okay? I am not sure that I would believe her, even if she were standing next to me right now. I said my farewells with a silent promise to visit more often.

I began to make my way to the opposite side of the yard. As I passed, I read off the names from the back of the stones in my mind. I recognized some of the family names. A couple of my high school friends were here. Tragic accidents had taken them well before their time.

My steps became leaden as I approached a particularly small headstone. I stopped about twenty yards away and stared at it. It was surrounded with flowers. Unbidden tears filled my eyes. People still remembered her, even after all this time. It touched my heart in a significant way.

I took a deep breath and crossed the remaining distance to where Kailey lay in eternal sleep. I blinked away more tears as I read the inscription on the stone.

In Loving Memory
Kailey Sophia Wayne
We Hold You Close Within Our Hearts

I knelt and placed the flowers I had brought on the ground next to the stone. I bowed my head and said a silent prayer for the daughter I never got to hold. Tears fell from my face to moisten the grass at my feet.

"I love you, Kailey." I did not need to say the words out loud, but it felt good to hear them in my own ears. "Your mom does, too. You would have been a perfect daughter. I know it. You will always be in my heart."

I stood and wiped the tears from my eyes. "Always remember that daddy loves you. I'll visit again soon."

I took one last look at the headstone with all the flowers around it. I gave a smile to all the things that might have been. I pictured Kailey taking her first steps before falling into Kara's arms. The excitement of her first day at school. Ferrying her to soccer practice and who knows what else. The joy of seeing her grow into a beautiful young woman. The feeling of satisfaction of watching her marry and have children of her own. All the days of her life that would never be.

I was glad that Kara had more children. I am sure it helped to ease the pain of losing a child. She could give her love to them and maybe forget for a while. I only had the dream of what Kailey might have been.

A breeze began to move through the nearby trees. It was as if the voices of those no longer able to speak were trying to tell me something. I shivered and turned away. The sound of the rustling leaves followed me all the way back to my car.

It was late afternoon when I left the cemetery and headed across town. I had not seen Kara since our night in my hotel room. I idly wondered if that was the work of her husband. I hoped it was not, but if I was honest with myself, I might do something similar if I was in his shoes. Nevertheless, I was going to try and see her before I headed back to California. I would never be able to live with myself if I gave her up without making a last appeal.

I spent the twenty minute drive to her house trying to think of what I might say to her that would change her mind. I had already poured my heart out to her. It had made no difference. I would not be a human being if I did not understand why she chose to stay with her husband. However, it did not change the fact that we both knew we were meant to be together. It would be a tragedy if we never fulfilled the promise of our lives.

The cloudless winter sky was bright and clear. The day held its feeble warmth despite the sun being past its zenith. The trees stretched their bare limbs upward in hope of finding new life. They swayed in a gentle breeze that promised better days to come. Hearts should not be broken on days such as these.

My time for thought ended as I pulled onto her street. I parked a couple blocks away from her house and took in the scene. It was a typical ranch-style house. It was large and appeared to be well maintained. A sizeable front yard wrapped around the side of the house to meet up with the back deck. I had to admit it was a nice place.

There were two vehicles parked in the driveway. It led me to believe that her husband was home. It was disappointing, as it would make it much more difficult to talk to her alone.

I sat in my car and contemplated my options. There were not many to choose from. I could wait and see if her husband left the house. The other option was to march right up to the porch and knock on the door. I was sure the second option would not end well. Fortunately, I got the chance I was looking for fifteen minutes later.

I saw the front door open and Kara stepped out onto the porch. She was dressed in blue jeans and a heavy green sweater. As luck would have it, she stepped down the three steps and headed for the mailbox that stood next to the road.

I watched as she reached the box and took out a couple pieces of mail. It was now or never. I got out of the car and shut the door. The sound of it closing brought her head up and she looked in my direction. The mail fell from her hands as her eyes found me.

My heart beat like an out of control drum. The

world faded away as my eyes locked on hers. All that existed was the reality of us. I willed her to feel the love I held in my heart for her. All the threads of my life were balanced in this one moment.

I tried to imagine what she was seeing. A tall man with wind-tousled hair standing in the middle of the road with his heart in his hands. A man with tears streaming down his face. A man who knew her as well as a man could know a woman. A man she knew so well.

She knew why I had come. It was the time of final decision. She took a couple steps toward me then stopped. My mind raced. *Oh, my Kara, make the decision. Come away with me. Let me love you. I love you.*

I stood in silence, my thoughts not finding voice. The words had all been said before. She knew my heart and I knew hers. It was her mind and sense of responsibility to her children that held her back.

I reached my hand out to her. She took a few more steps before stopping again. She was half way to me. I could see her chest heaving with the effort of crying.

I finally spoke, but the voice did not sound like my own. It sounded a million miles away. It took all

I had to simply say, "Kara."

She could not hear me, but she saw me speak her name. Her shoulders shook with each sob that escaped her. My knees buckled when I saw her say my name in return. I leaned on the car door to prevent myself from falling to my knees.

I had nothing left. My soul was spent. My heart had been poured out and was now empty. All I could do was whisper, "I love you. I love you."

A smile formed through her tears. It kindled a sliver of hope within me. She began to take another step, but she then turned her head back toward the house. I looked past her to the porch where I saw her husband step into view. Their youngest daughter was alongside. He seemed to be looking for Kara but had not spotted her yet.

Kara turned back to me. The smile on her face now replaced with a profound look of sadness. She shook her head and I could see her say the words, "I'm sorry."

It was then that my world shattered into a thousand pieces. Our lives had danced on a knife's edge, and the second half of my soul had just been cut away. It is a strange thing to feel your soul tear apart. I knew that I would never again be a complete person.

Our gazes locked for one final time. We each sent a lifetime of love across that spiritual connection. We had no allusions as to the heartbreak that was to come.

It was all more than I could take. I gave her one final smile before I lowered my head and climbed back into the car. I started the engine, put the transmission into gear, and made a slow U-turn in the road. She was still standing there when I stopped and peered through the rearview mirror. She watched me with those angelic, light sapphire eyes.

I sat and studied her through my tears for a long moment. It took everything I had to remove my foot from the brake and put the car into motion. The road to salvation was behind me. The path to damnation ahead.

My last sight of Kara, as she receded in the distance, was one in which her beautiful face was covered by her shaking hands. A moment later she was gone.

I did not see her again until she arrived at Harrison Manor. Thirty years later.

15

DECEMBER 18TH

The memories faded from my eyes as my mind returned to the present. My heart did not know how to feel. My body was half filled with joy and half sorrow. These emotions flowed through my veins until they mixed to become something else. It was when I glanced at Kara that I knew what it was. It was resignation.

I did not need to ask her to know she had been reliving the same memories in her own mind. I suspected the look on her face mirrored my own. It was the look of someone who had tallied up the happy and sad moments and found the balance heavily weighted in the wrong direction. Now here we were, at the end of our lives, with no time left to correct it.

Kara's eyes slowly closed and I thought she had

gone to sleep. They soon fluttered open again to look directly at me. Her voice was very faint. "I don't have much time."

A shock of panic flared through me. I touched a hand to her forehead to find she was icy cold. Her skin had become paler than ever before. Nancy came running up to check on Kara. She must have been watching us from the trees.

She took in the situation with a quick glance. A look of concern crossed her face. "We need to get her back to the nursing home. Now!"

Kara shook her head. "No."

Nancy ignored her. She looked at me. "I will come back for you later. I need to get her back as soon as possible."

She began to push Kara's wheelchair away from me. Astonishingly, Kara found some inner reserve of strength. Her hand shot up and latched onto Nancy's arm with a firm grip. The strength in her voice returned. "No! I will stay here!"

The surprised nurse abruptly stopped. "Kara, you are not well. We need to get you back to your bed."

Kara turned to me with pleading eyes. I nearly melted into the ground. She was not going anywhere.

I stepped closer. "Nancy, Kara is staying here with me. Do you remember what I said to you earlier?" I hoped she recalled what I had said about it being the last time.

Nancy gave me a withering gaze. She was torn between caring for her patient and allowing the patient to do what she wanted. For a moment, I thought she might defy me, but her head finally lowered as she yielded to our wishes.

Her voice sounded tired. "Okay, Kara. What is it you want me to do?"

Kara's hand dropped to her lap. It was if she had expended all the energy she had left in that one gesture. The strength had dissipated from her voice, as well. "Take me down to the pond."

Nancy shook her head but said nothing. She turned the wheelchair around and pointed it toward the pond. I followed reluctantly at their side. A dark shadow was looming above me. I did not want to face it.

We stopped at a bench that sat near the water's edge. I sat down as Nancy stepped away. She stayed closer to Kara this time. So be it. She would be witness to what was to come.

I reached down and plucked a stone from the ground. The stone left my hand as I made a sidearm throw. It skipped across the water several times before sinking below the surface. Each skip left a ring of ripples that widened out to spread across the pond. It was if each ring was a signpost of our lives. Each memory rippled across the water to mix with the pale blue reflection of the sky. The breathtaking remembrances of a fading life were left shrouded and unclear as they disappeared into the distance.

I felt the beginning of a breeze on my face. I looked up at the trees as the leaves began to tremble. The silent voices had returned. I tried to hear what they were saying, but it was just out of reach. I felt that I would know their message soon enough.

I glanced at Kara. I could see that she was having difficulty holding up her head. She was weakening with each minute that passed. Her voice had returned to a whisper. "My life is not what I thought it would be. I lived a stranger's life."

I took her hand and tried to keep the tears a bay. "I'm sorry, honey. I know you had hopes and dreams. I'm sorry that I could not give them to you."

She raised her eyes to the sky. "Fate, it seems, had other plans. I thought it would be the two of us, together, for our entire lives. Did you?"

I answered as her eyes lowered to look at me. "Yes, I did. I thought nothing would separate us."

She gave my hand a gentle squeeze. "Do you remember the first time I ever spoke to you?"

That brought a happy smile to my face. "How could I forget? You kissed me on the cheek."

She returned my smile with a slight one of her own. "I knew on the bus ride home that I was going to marry you."

My mood sobered a little. "I wish we had."

"Me, too."

I turned away as tears began to fill my eyes again. I peered across the pond and saw two ducks swimming across the frigid water. I wondered what they were doing here in the middle of winter. Was the history of their lives weighing them down, too? They swam into the cattails that ringed the edge of the pond. The reeds swayed back and forth in the breeze as if in a trance. They were silent spectators to my growing grief.

Kara's voice brought me out of my reverie. It had weakened even more. "Nothing that has happened will ever change the fact that you are my one true love. I want you to remember that. As long as you live, never forget what you are to me."

I wanted to say so many things to her. Time was short, so I said what mattered most. "You are the love of my life. You are the brightest star in my sky. My heart beats because of you. It is where you will always remain."

She leaned her head back so that it rested on the back of her wheelchair. There were tears in her eyes, too. I could hear what sounded like wonder in her voice. "I no longer feel like I'm floating as if I were a cloud. I am the cloud. I must go now."

I cried out in anguish. "Kara! Don't go!" I gripped her hand as tightly as I could in an attempt to keep her here with me. "I love you with all my heart. Take that with you if you must go. You are my dearest love."

Her head suddenly rose up and her eyes sharpened their focus on me. I could barely hear her above the breeze. "I will take your love wherever I go. I love you." She paused to study me. It seemed as though she were trying to memorize my face. Her head began to waiver. It was a struggle for her to speak the next words. "Happy Birthday."

Tears flowed down my cheeks as I leaned in to kiss her. It was a lingering kiss that did not end until

I felt her body relax.

When I pulled away, I could see that the life had gone out of her light sapphire eyes.

16

DECEMBER 19TH

I found myself looking down at the white porcelain of a sink. I did not remember getting up and walking to the bathroom. I had turned on the water, but I did not remember doing that, either. Steam was rising from where the hot water was gathering in the bowl. It fogged the surface of the mirror that hung above it. My outline in the mirror was shadowed and indistinct. It was exactly how my soul felt. I reached over and pulled a towel from where it hung on a peg on the wall. With great deliberation, I wiped the steam from the surface of the glass.

I looked at myself and was saddened by what I saw. The gaunt face of an old man reflected back at me. His head was topped with a few strands of gray hair. His skin was spotted and pale. He looked so frail and inconsequential that I thought he might fade away. His reflection was echoed in green eyes that were tired from seeing too much of life.

There was a hint of something more. I tried to capture it, but it was hidden behind layers of a life lived. I leaned in closer and looked long and hard. The face of a young man began to slowly appear before me. I remembered him. He had been so full of hopes and dreams. He had known his future and ran toward it. He was the man who had fallen in love with Kara Wayne. Yet now he was the man who knew a great love and a great loss. A thankful man with a heart full of regret.

The beauty and tragedy of my life spun around me like wisps of smoke. The memories were fading in and out of view at the whim of the wind…

I saw the first time she smiled at me. Our first date. The night when she ran into my arms and told me she was pregnant. The loss of our child. The devastation when she told me that she did not love me anymore. My birthday party. The last time we made love.

They came and went, each memory taking a tiny part of myself with it as they disappeared into the ether. They touched my mind in equal parts joy and pain. I would give anything to go back and do it again. To go back and correct the one tiny moment that changed everything. But I can't, and that may be the greatest tragedy of all.

I felt so tired. I wondered if I had the strength to go on. I wondered if I wanted to.

Kara had given me the most precious gift any person can give another. Her death. Being there at her concluding moment was my greatest gift to her. We shared that beautiful release with each other. After all we had been through, it could not have been any other way.

These thoughts of her threatened to overwhelm me with grief. What was I going to do now? Even though we had spent most of our lives apart, I always knew she was out there somewhere. Now she is gone and with her went all my love. I no longer had anything to dream about.

I remembered a song, now ancient with time, which stirred my heart with its familiarity. Its ending verse says more than I ever could about my life with Kara.

If it takes my whole life
I won't break, I won't bend
It will all be worth it
Worth it in the end
'Cause I can only tell you what I know
That I need you in my life
And when the stars have all gone out
You'll still be burning so bright.
Cast me gently into morning
For the night has been unkind.

EPILOGUE

To: Kara Wayne's Children
    Caitlyn, Sara, John

My name is Nancy Ferrell. I work at Harrison Manor, the nursing home where Kara spent her last few years. I wasn't sure if I should write you, but after going over it in my mind for a few days, I decided that I can't keep silent. This story needs to be told.

Kara was one of my patients. I looked after her for the three years she spent with us. Her medical prognosis wasn't good when she arrived. The doctor's said that she might live another six months. It was an optimistic estimation. All of the employees at Harrison Manor were amazed that she held on for so long. They thought it was some kind of miracle. This is the reason I am writing you this letter.

In truth, it *was* a miracle that she lived as long as she did. The miracle didn't come from God or medical science. It came in the form of another resident of the Manor. His name was Evan Pike. I'm sure you know him, because he sat at her bedside every day that she lived. You couldn't see Kara without seeing him. They made a pretense of just being friends, but those of us who were around them every day, knew the truth.

It was evident from the first day she arrived at the Manor that they had a connection. I remember some of her family wondering why she chose to come here instead of a nursing home closer to where she lived. Evan was the reason.

He was at her side on that first day and rarely left her for more than a few minutes at a time. They ate every meal together, participated in every event together, and held hands every moment they could. It nearly brought me to tears each day to see the love shining in their eyes. To see two elderly people love so intensely gave hope to us all for our own futures.

Evan said that Kara never told you about their relationship. Their story is a very passionate, yet tragic one. They met in high school, fell in love, and had every intention of getting married. They were going to have a child and live their lives together. They both soon learned that the world can be a cruel place. A place where chance and fate play tricks on us all. They were separated, and by the time they found each other again, life had too firm a grip on Kara. They would never fully find their way back to each other, even though it was the one thing they wanted most.

Please don't misunderstand. Evan told me Kara loved you very much. You are the reason she stayed all those years. She chose your happiness over hers. A mother's ultimate sacrifice. It broke his heart, and maybe hers, too. As I said, sometimes life has too firm a grip.

Kara passed away on his birthday. Evan passed two days later. He came to me the night before he died and told me their entire story. I believe he had been thinking about doing this for quite some time. He brought a recording device with him so that I could record everything he said. I have included a copy of the recording with this letter.

I think he felt a need for someone to carry their memory onward. I gathered from what he told me that very few people knew or suspected the feelings they had for one another. This letter and the recording may shock you. Nevertheless, you need to know what they did for each other.

What I'm trying to tell you, is that they both would have died within months of Kara's arrival, if it wasn't for the love they shared. It sustained them. It gave them strength to fight another day. Love might not have healed their cancers, but it kept it at bay for much longer than anyone could have imagined. They each fought with everything they had to make it to another day because it meant another day together.

You may be thinking the same thing I had when he told me their story. How can a man, for his entire life, love a woman he couldn't be with? I asked him as much, and his answer was a predictably sad one.

He said there were other women. A couple of the relationships were good enough to keep them going for a few years. He never found them fulfilling enough to make them last. It was impossible for him to love anyone the way he loved Kara. He knew their love remained, even when she turned him away. In the end, he never married nor had children. He cried for a long time after he told me that. I cried with him.

I'm sure it's difficult for you to read this letter.

I'm sorry if these words hurt you. If you take away only one thing from them, let it be this: They saved each others lives every day for three years. Evan gave you that much more time with your mother. I hope, in some small way, you can find it in your heart to thank him for that.

Sincerely,

Nancy Ferrell
Head Nurse
Harrison Manor Nursing Home

Kevin Teague

THE END